I0600656

GUIDE TO MULTI ASSET- FUND MANAGEMENT

BROKEN

How Full-Stack Venture Capital Funds™ Will Fix
the Broken Venture Capital Industry

By
MICHAEL 'Q' QUATRINI
CEO/CIO, CAPITAL Q® VENTURES

B R O K E N
Disclaimer

The information presented in this book is based on the author's research, professional experience, analysis, and informed opinion. While every effort has been made to ensure accuracy, completeness, and clarity, no representations or warranties are made regarding the accuracy or applicability of the information contained herein, nor the financial outcomes that may result from the use of any concepts, strategies, or opinions discussed.

This book is provided for informational and educational purposes only and is not intended as, and should not be construed to be, legal, tax, investment, financial, or other professional advice. Readers should consult with their own legal, tax, financial, or investment advisors before making any decisions based on the information in this book.

The author and publisher expressly disclaim any liability for financial loss, economic harm, or other damages—whether direct or indirect—that may result from the use, application, or reliance upon the information contained in this work.

Any diagrams, charts, or illustrations included in this book are simplified and conceptual in nature. They are intended solely to support the discussion of key ideas and should not be interpreted as representations of actual fund structures, investment vehicles, operations, or regulatory frameworks.

B R O K E N

For permission requests, contact the publisher at:
100 East Faith Terrace, Suite 1016
Maitland, FL 32751

Additional Notices

FIRST EDITION — 2025

Library of Congress Cataloging-in-Publication Data:
2026902305

Case ID 1-15086458241 Paperback

ISBN 979-8-9948389-1-4

Table of Contents

Forward

Since 2021, the world of entrepreneurship and investing has transformed dramatically. Economic shifts, market volatility, and evolving investor expectations have reshaped how private and public companies are built and funded. In this dynamic landscape, *Broken* emerges as a must-read for entrepreneurs and venture capitalists alike. The author delivers a compelling guide that addresses the new realities of business creation, offering actionable insights for founders navigating fundraising, hiring, and scaling, and urging investors to rethink traditional approaches to better align with entrepreneurs.

This book's relevance lies in its clarity and foresight. It unpacks the complexities of today's markets, where rapid technological advancements and global uncertainties demand adaptability. For entrepreneurs, it provides a blueprint for avoiding common pitfalls, whether securing capital, pivoting strategies in a dynamic international market, or building resilient, sustainable teams. For venture capitalists, it challenges outdated models and advocates an alignment of incentives that prioritizes mutual trust and long-term value over short-term gains. Quatrini's ability to distill these principles into practical strategies makes this work essential for anyone serious about investing in, building a company in a highly competitive global market.

B R O K E N

As a global experience entrepreneur, investing, building, and acquiring technology solutions across the world in energy, fintech, payments, and the Digital Asset Industry, I found *Quatrini's Broken* both a wake-up call and a roadmap for any dynamic leader. Its emphasis on aligning founder and investor goals resonates deeply in a time when missteps can be costly and unforgiving. The book's insights are grounded yet forward-thinking, offering a fresh perspective on navigating the post-2021 business world. It's a call to action for founders to approach their ventures with strategic clarity and for investors to foster partnerships that drive sustainable growth by aligning incentives.

In a world where change is the only constant, *Broken* is a vital resource. It equips readers with the tools to thrive amid uncertainty, making it indispensable for anyone looking to build or invest in the next generation of companies. Read it before you take your next step…it will redefine how you approach the journey.

, Gary Cardone, Entrepreneur, Investor, Disruptor

About Gary Cardone

Gary Cardone is a global entrepreneur, investor, and Managing Partner of Card1Ventures, where he focuses on blockchain technology, digital assets, and next-generation financial infrastructure.

Born and raised in Lake Charles, Louisiana, Cardone began his career in energy markets, joining Natural Gas

Clearinghouse (later Dynegy) as its twelfth employee. Over the next fifteen years, he helped transform it into a Fortune 30 company, and Cardone became known as one of Europe's most successful trading executives, pioneering the UK's National Balancing Point, which remains one of the world's most reliable energy trading hubs.

After retiring from energy trading in 2002, Cardone returned to the United States, serving as a strategic adviser to major private equity and infrastructure firms, including Arclight Capital. He later became a seed investor in Cardone Capital, founded by his twin brother, Grant Cardone, which is one of the largest independent owners of multifamily real estate in the country. In 2012 Cardone co-founded Chargebacks911, the leading fraud and dispute technology provider to global banks and payment processors.

Today, through Card1Ventures, Cardone invests in high-growth technology and digital asset companies such as Node40, an industry leader in blockchain accounting and compliance. A lifelong entrepreneur and mentor, he continues to advise founders and investors on building profitable, sustainable ventures.

He resides in the Tampa Bay area and remains an avid skier, fisherman, and student of history.

Introduction

"How is Venture Capital Broken?"

I remember the first time I sat across the table from a venture capitalist, one of the coastal titans with a Patagonia vest and a vocabulary full of acronyms. It was 2005, and while I had grown my family office from strategic exits and golden parachutes, I was green enough in the Venture Capital and the VC industry to still think that "Series A" meant someone was bringing the good wine.

We were discussing a startup founder I had invested in and was helping mentor. Somewhere between the term sheet gymnastics and his third explanation that "this is standard," I had a quiet realization: This traditional VC model was built to spotlight the investments and the fund's investment process over the needs of the actual investors in Venture Capital funds.

Don't get me wrong, Venture Capital has its legends. It has funded moonshots, rewritten industries, and minted billionaires. But lately, by lately, I mean the last 3 to 5 years, something has gone off-script. The headlines still trumpet unicorns, but the reality is that successful startup exits are becoming rare. The spreadsheets still promise 10x returns, but Investors are seeing "liquidity" the way I see my abs: quite theoretical.

B R O K E N

This book isn't a hit piece. It's a eulogy, of sorts, a respectful farewell to an old model that had its moment and a welcome to what must come next: a more adaptable, more rational, and more exhaustive approach to innovation capital.

What's Broken?

Venture funds today are trapped in a time warp:

- They raise capital every 3 to 4 years in a cycle designed for a 7-to-10-year liquidity horizon.

- They chase growth at any cost, ignore cash flow, and pray for a Series D and now maybe even Series E and F.

- They build portfolios like blackjack players, knowing many bets will bust, but in the hopes a few aces pay for the night.

For most fund managers, success now means beating a benchmark that no longer reflects reality. For founders, it often means chasing a capital stack that grows taller while their ownership shrinks. And for limited partners, it means a lot of waiting, waiting for exits. Waiting for liquidity. Waiting for a pitch deck that doesn't use "AI" seventeen times without actually explaining how it works.

What's Better?

Over the past decade, I've had the golden opportunity to work across venture capital, private equity, and private credit; not because I'm indecisive, but because I've come to believe they belong together. Like tequila, lime juice, and triple sec: each one is fine on its own, but together? Now we're talking. Or, as they say in Margaritaville, ahora estamos hablando.

In this book, I'll argue that the future of Venture Capital investing doesn't live in a single asset class. It lives in a Full-Stack Venture Capital Fund which is a multi-asset fund that blends the best of three worlds:

- Venture Capital, for its upside.

- Private Credit, for its income and structure.

- Private Equity, for its control and long-term value creation.

This isn't theory. It's happening; quietly, methodically, and when done right, profitably. There are firms (mine included, though we'll get to that in the Epilogue) that are building funds where founders get to scale without surrender, investors get real yield without a 12-year wait, and communities see real, measurable outcomes that don't require being acquired, ringing a bell, or a SPAC announcement to validate their worth.

Why This Matters Now?

We're entering an age in which capital must be strategically allocated, quickly adaptable, and transparently managed. Inflation has returned. Interest rates aren't going back to zero. The traditional "spray and pray" VC model is looking more like "spray and delay." And in a market where liquidity is king and diversification is armor, being a one-trick pony is an expensive way to go extinct.

So, welcome. If you've ever wondered why your investor updates feel more like therapy sessions, or why your portfolio companies are burning money like it's 2021, you're not alone.

Let's talk about what comes next.

Thesis Statement

Traditional Venture Capital is experiencing major hurdles that suggest it may be reaching a structural dead-end. Liquidity constraints, fund misalignment, and a binary risk profile have collectively reduced the model's effectiveness for both investors and founders. In response to these challenges, a new future is emerging that combines Venture Capital, Private Credit, and Private Equity into a single, adaptive, Full-Stack Venture Capital Funds™ model, which is a multi-asset fund with unique organizational characteristics, including a mentoring mandate for its portfolio companies. This model is designed to offer sustainable returns, strategic flexibility, and system-wide value creation, addressing the current limitations of traditional Venture Capital funds.

Chapter 1

The Cracks in the Capital Stack

Before I jump on my soapbox, I want to be clear: "I love Venture Capital!"

It's what gets me out of bed every morning. I believe, deeply, that Venture Capital is one of the most vital engines of growth in any free economy. Here in the U.S., and increasingly around the world, it is the *"Lifeblood"* of innovation and a foundational pillar of the entrepreneurial ecosystem.

So, before we dive into what's broken, let's acknowledge what's working, and why Venture Capital remains so vitally important:

- **It fuels innovation.** VC funding allows companies to develop and commercialize groundbreaking technologies and disruptive ideas across nearly every sector.

- **It supports startups.** Especially those with unproven business models who would never get a bank loan.

VCs take early-stage risk and help those founders grow.

- **It drives economic growth and job creation.** Many of the companies that define our modern economy, platforms, tools, and marketplaces were backed by venture. That means new jobs, new industries, and entirely new categories of demand.

- **It brings expertise, not just capital.** The best VCs offer mentorship, operational support, and powerful networks. The money matters, but the strategic guidance can be even more valuable.

Venture Capital, at its best, acts as a catalyst, transforming ideas into companies, and companies into movements that push entire industries forward.

And it's not hyperbole to say that nearly every modern tech billionaire minted in the late 20th and early 21st century scaled their company with the help of Venture Capital. We're talking about household names, the people who built world-changing businesses:

1. **Bill Gates (Microsoft):** While Gates bootstrapped early on, Microsoft received a $1 million venture investment from Technology Venture Investors

(TVI) in 1981, which was critical fuel for its early growth.

2. **Steve Jobs (Apple):** In 1977, Apple secured $91,000 from Mike Markkula, a former Intel exec. That led to institutional investments from Venrock, one of the earliest VC powerhouses.

3. **Jeff Bezos (Amazon):** Sure, his parents wrote the first checks, but in 1996, Kleiner Perkins Caufield & Byers invested $8 million, which was a cornerstone of Amazon's rapid rise.

4. **Larry Page & Sergey Brin (Google):** In 1999, Sequoia and Kleiner Perkins co-led a $25 million Series A. That wasn't just money; it was rocket fuel.

5. **Elon Musk (PayPal, Tesla, SpaceX):** Even though Musk reinvested his own PayPal proceeds, institutional VC played a major role in scaling Tesla and SpaceX into category-defining giants.

So yes, Venture Capital is essential. It's launched legends, reshaped economies, and moved humanity forward. But loving something doesn't mean being blind to its flaws. And that's where this book begins.

B R O K E N

Part 1: Welcome to the Hangover

If you've ever looked at a startup's cap table after four funding rounds and thought, "Wow, there's not a lot of room left for the founders," you're not alone. The Venture Capital ecosystem, which once prided itself on risk-taking, innovation, and partnerships, has become ironically risk-averse in structure, conventional in thinking, and increasingly extractive in practice. The cracks in the capital stack aren't theoretical. They are structural and worsening.

But this didn't happen overnight. Like most systemic unraveling, it began slowly, then suddenly. You could argue it began years ago, but the inflection point, at least for this cycle, was the COVID-fueled bull run that left everyone feeling wealthier, smarter, and bolder than they actually were. Investors committed record-breaking capital. VCs opened their fund decks with confidence and FOMO. Founders raised at fantasy valuations for businesses with more slide deck pages than customers.

And then came 2022.

If 2020 was the champagne bottle, and 2021 was the confetti, then 2022 was the morning after, a cold slap of valuation resets, exit freezes, and down rounds so sharp they had lawyers searching for anti-dilution clauses like buried treasure. By 2023, nobody was pretending anymore. Unicorns quietly became donkeys. The IPO market slammed shut. And private markets began pricing in what public markets already knew: capital isn't free. VCs started seeking "Cockroaches," or startups that would survive any disaster, rather than the previous, highly coveted "Unicorns" with valuations starting with a "B".

This chapter isn't just about the symptoms. It's about the mechanics behind the breakdown. If we want to fix the future of Venture Capital, we need to understand why the present is broken. Let's start by unpacking what happened post-pandemic, and why it exposed the vulnerabilities baked into the traditional VC model.

The Post-Pandemic Reckoning

In 2020, everyone panicked… for about 4 weeks. Then something strange happened. The market took off like a rocket. Stimulus checks, zero interest rates, and an unprecedented surge in liquidity created a risk-on environment so aggressive that the term "due diligence" briefly trended toward extinction.

A founder with a solid LinkedIn and an NFT deck could raise millions. Tiger Global and SoftBank were cutting checks at lightning speed. Seed rounds swelled to Series A sizes. Series A rounds looked like Series C. Nobody wanted to miss out on the next big thing.

But the absolute risk wasn't just in overpaying. It was in the capital structure mismatch between what funds promised their Investors and what the market could reasonably deliver over time. Fund Managers were underwriting long-dated, illiquid bets while still operating on short-term optics: paper markups, growth-at-all-costs narratives, and a mythical exit horizon that always seemed just five years away.

When the macro tides turned, it exposed the rot beneath the growth stories. Suddenly, unit economics mattered again. Burn multiples were scrutinized. Companies once seen as darlings of disruption were now just expensive experiments with no clear path to profitability. Many still are.

As Investors watched markdowns pile up and exits evaporate, they began to question what exactly they had bought into. And many didn't like the answer.

Structural Misalignment and the False Promise of Liquidity

Here's the dirty little secret about venture capital: most Investors don't really understand how long they're going to wait to see their money again. They're told to expect a 10-year fund life, but what they get is more like 12 to 15 years of capital calls, quarterly PDFs, delays, and excuses.

VCs are incentivized to markup unrealized portfolio positions because it makes their fund performance look greater. But Distributions to Paid-In Capital (DPI) or actual money returned to investors is what matter. And that's the number that's been increasingly hard to justify.

You'd think, with all the unicorns minted during the last cycle, investors would be flush with cash. But most of those companies haven't exited. And many of those that have done so in ways that destroyed valuation rather than rewarded it.

Think of WeWork. Think of Instacart. Think of any SPAC deal that traded at $10 and now trade below $2. The illusion of liquidity was just that, an illusion. The window shut, and most funds were caught holding bags that nobody wanted to claim.

In Part 2, we'll unpack why diversification in a single asset class creates false comfort and examine how most VC portfolios are far more correlated than fund managers like to admit.

Part 2: The Illusion of Diversification

Ask a traditional venture capitalist how they manage risk, and you'll likely hear the same answer: diversification. The logic is simple. If you invest in 20 to 30 companies, you can afford to have a few flame-outs. One or two big wins should carry the fund.

It's a tidy story. But like many tidy stories in finance, it starts to fall apart under scrutiny.

The problem isn't the idea of diversification. The problem is that most VC portfolios are diversified in name only. Sure, they may hold 25 startups across different industries. Some are in enterprise SaaS, others in fintech, others in consumer goods. But when you step back, most of them are early-stage, venture-backed startups that rely on the same macroeconomic conditions to thrive and create harvest strategies or the elusive "exit".

That's not diversification. That's correlation dressed in a hoodie.

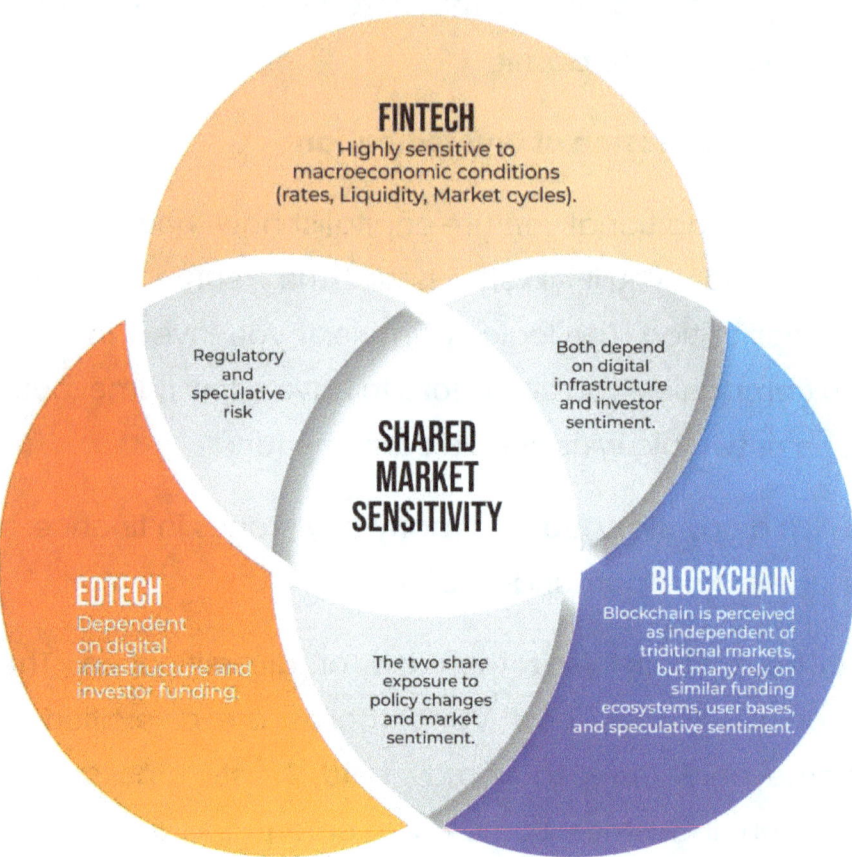

Fintech, Edtech, and Blockchain may appear diversified on the surface, but their shared dependencies on macroeconomic conditions, liquidity cycles, sentiment-driven markets, and regulatory shifts create high correlation risk. This diagram illustrates how

When the IPO market is strong and M&A is flowing, all boats rise. When capital is cheap and growth is rewarded over profitability, every company looks like a winner. But when the tide goes out, they all struggle at once.

This is especially dangerous when paired with the obsession over hitting "home runs." Most funds aren't trying to produce consistent singles and doubles. They're swinging for the fences on every at-bat. That mentality works great when a few companies hit $1 billion exits. But when exits stall, and no one's buying, you're stuck with a portfolio full of overvalued companies that all need more cash at the worst possible time.

When Your Diversification Is Just Duplicated Risk

Let's take a fictional example. Say you have a VC fund with 25 portfolio companies. The fund has exposure to healthcare tech, edtech, logistics platforms, blockchain infrastructure, and two food delivery apps. Sounds diversified, right?

But look closer.

Every one of these companies is:

• Pre-profit
• Venture-backed
• Dependent on future fundraising
• Built for acquisition or IPO
• Valued using discounted future cash flows (many with no cash flow)

• Highly sensitive to the cost of capital and the exit environment

Now imagine a macro environment where:

• Interest rates rise
• The IPO market shuts down
• Public valuations fall
• Corporate acquirers freeze spending
• Investors tighten commitments

Suddenly, your entire portfolio is underwater. That edtech startup that looked like a rocket ship? Now it's a 70-person company with no revenue and an upcoming bridge round that no one wants to lead. The blockchain play? It's pivoted to AI, then to carbon credits, and now it's just pivoting for sport.

Diversification only works when the risks aren't correlated. But in Venture Capital, the biggest risk isn't that one startup fails. It's that the entire market environment shifts against you and every one of your companies gets caught in the downdraft at the same time.

Everyone Is Waiting for the Same Exit Door

One of the worst-kept secrets in VC is that everyone is waiting for the same exit. The whole strategy hinges on someone else buying the company. That's it. You either go public or get acquired. Those are the doors. And when both are closed, the model doesn't just suffer. It seizes.

Unlike private equity, which can extract value from cash-flowing businesses through operational improvements, or private credit, which earns a return the moment the check clears, VC requires a specific type of liquidity event to generate returns.

That might have worked in the 2010s when low rates fueled a boom in corporate M&A and public markets welcomed tech companies with open arms. But in today's tighter environment, that same reliance on exit timing looks less like a strategy and more like a coin toss.

Worse still, these liquidity assumptions are hardcoded into fund models. Fund Managers pitch their funds on the assumption that 2x or 3x outcomes will occur within 7 to 10 years. But if market conditions push exits out by another 3 to 5 years, the fund's entire Internal Rate of Return (IRR) profile collapses. Investors aren't just waiting longer. They're earning less.

No Cushion, No Control

What makes it even more precarious is how little structural protection VCs have in the capital stack. Equity holders are last in line. If a company falters or is sold at a discount, the common and preferred shareholders are often left with pennies or worse, paperwork. There's no yield, or coupon to clip along the way, no collateral, no redemption rights. The whole bet is backloaded. And while Fund Managers can charge fees and collect carry on paper gains, Investors get to enjoy the long, quiet suspense of watching those marks decay.

In Part 3, we'll turn to the institutional side and explore why Investors are quietly walking away from traditional VC, and how their priorities have shifted toward liquidity, yield, and capital efficiency.

Part 3: Why Institutional Investors Are Pulling Back

The capital behind Venture Capital is shifting. Quietly, steadily, and with more calculation than emotion, institutional investors, the real clients of any venture fund, are reevaluating their commitments to pure-play VC.

Some are scaling back. Some are pausing altogether. A few are even whispering the word "never again." And this isn't a reaction to a single bad quarter or a rough year. This is a correction rooted in structural disappointment and strategic reprioritization.

When DPI Doesn't Show Up

Distributions to Paid-In Capital (DPI) is the one metric that cuts through the fog of Venture Capital performance.

You can mark up your NAV, write glowing quarterly letters, host exclusive investor meetings at Napa vineyards, and tell everyone your portfolio is up 3x on paper. But if you're not returning cash to your Investors, you are not delivering.

Investors know this…and they've been patient, but they are also fiduciaries. University endowments, pension funds, foundations, and sovereign wealth managers have obligations, real ones with timelines. You can't fund scholarships or pay retirees with marked-up SAFEs. You need liquidity.

Over the past five years, traditional VC has underdelivered on DPI. The paper gains haven't been converted into actual returns. And worse, the timing of those returns has extended well beyond original projections. Some funds from 2012 and 2014 are still open, still waiting for their "big exits."

When a fund crosses the decade mark and hasn't distributed meaningful capital, Investors stop seeing it as a return vehicle and start seeing it as an annuity for the GP.

The Re-up Problem

Most Investors don't invest in a single venture fund. They commit to a manager and often sign up for a series of funds over time. This creates a delicate balancing act. You're committing new capital every few years while still waiting to see the outcome from funds that are years, even decades, away from meaningful realization. This couples with paper valuation increases that feed into the target allocation percentage makes it difficult to deploy new calital to those traditions VC funds.

This is the re-up problem. And it's become a growing source of tension.

In theory, if the older funds were performing well and generating distributions, it's easy to recommit. But if capital is locked up, DPI is low, and market conditions make future exits look bleak, then the next fund commitment starts to feel like throwing good money after bad.

Many Investors now feel overexposed to venture, not just in dollar terms but in duration risk. They've committed to multiple vintages, all built on similar assumptions, and all vulnerable to the same macro cycles. Without exits to create breathing room, they're simply too full.

The Real Cost of Venture Capital

One often overlooked element is the cost of capital allocation itself. Venture funds are expensive, not just in fees but in opportunity cost.

While a traditional 2 and 20 fee structure is well understood, the blind pool nature of VC means Investors commit capital up front but have little to no say in how it's deployed or when it's returned. That lack of control, when paired with lagging DPI, makes the asset class less appealing compared to more modern vehicles like co-investment platforms, direct lending funds, or even secondary funds with more defined timelines.

And unlike private equity, which can often return capital through dividends, recapitalizations, or interim sales, venture funds offer no such partial returns. You wait, or you walk away empty.

Institutional Investors have begun to reassess whether the expected upside of Venture Capital is worth the certainty of illiquidity. Increasingly, the answer is no.

A Shift Toward Yield and Flexibility

This shift isn't emotional. It's mechanical. When inflation crept back into the economy and rates rose from zero to something resembling normal, the entire investment universe was repriced.

Suddenly, private credit was yielding 10 to 12 percent with real collateral. Real estate, infrastructure, and income-focused funds became attractive again. Liquidity became valuable in a way it hadn't been in over a decade.

For a large institution managing billions, allocating capital to an illiquid, long-dated vehicle like Venture Capital became a harder sell. Why take that risk when safer, yield-generating strategies were finally back on the menu?

Even those who still believe in venture are looking to access it differently through continuation funds, secondaries, and multi-asset structures that reduce single-strategy risk.

Conversations Are Changing

I've sat in those LP meetings. I've heard the shift in tone.

Five years ago, the questions were about growth rates, valuation upticks, and how to get access to top-tier managers.

Today, the questions are about cash flow modeling, downside protection, liquidity management, and duration compression.

This isn't just a weather change. It's climate change. And Venture Capital managers who ignore it do so at their peril.

In Part 4, we'll explore how delayed exits and frozen liquidity windows are eroding fund performance metrics like IRR and DPI, and why the traditional venture timeline is now fundamentally out of sync with investor expectations.

Part 4: Liquidity, Delayed Exits, and the Venture Math Problem

For a Venture Capital fund to be considered successful, it used to need just one thing: a good story. If you had a few strong markups, a well-known logo on the cap table, and maybe a TechCrunch article about your portfolio's breakout startup, you were golden. Actual exits were treated like an eventuality...they will come...just wait.

But stories don't pay investors. Liquidity does.

And the longer the story drags on, the more the math turns against you.

The IRR Trap

Most Investors use the Internal Rate of Return (IRR) as one of their core metrics for evaluating fund performance. On paper, IRR is elegant. It captures the time value of money, accounting for how quickly capital returns and how much of it does. In practice, though, IRR can be gamed and distorted, especially in a world where exits are delayed and unrealized gains dominate fund NAV.

Let's take two scenarios.

In Fund A, a $10 million investment returns $30 million in four years.

In Fund B, the same $10 million returns $45 million, but over 10 years.

Which one performs better?

From a multiple standpoint, Fund B wins. A 4.5x return beats a 3x. But from an IRR standpoint, Fund A is far superior. The faster return has a compounding advantage. That's what Investors are often chasing, not just absolute gains, but timely gains.

The problem is, most venture funds are trending toward the Fund B profile. The exits are taking longer. The returns are backloaded. And as a result, the IRR profile is collapsing even for funds with paper winners.

The DPI Illusion

DPI, or Distributions to Paid-In Capital, is the real scoreboard. It shows how much money has been returned to investors relative to what they invested.

A DPI of 1.0x means you got your original capital back. 1.5x means you've earned a 50 percent return in actual dollars. Most Investors target funds that will eventually return 2.0x or more.

But here's the catch: DPI doesn't care about paper value. If you invested $10 million, and your fund's NAV shows $50 million, but you've only gotten $1 million back in distributions, your DPI is still 0.1x. And until that NAV converts to cash, your return is imaginary.

In the current environment, many venture funds are DPI-poor and NAV-rich. That's not a sustainable condition.

The Compounding Cost of Delay

Every year a fund remains illiquid, the IRR drops. Every delay in exit erodes the time advantage that made the venture attractive in the first place. Remember, VC isn't about steady compounding. It's about spikes. You need those spikes to happen quickly. When they don't, the math turns ugly.

Here's how.

Let's say a venture fund projects a 3x return over ten years. That sounds decent. But if the big exits don't happen until year twelve or fifteen, the IRR could drop below 10 percent. For many Investors, that's below hurdle rate territory. And if inflation-adjusted expectations rise, that return becomes even less compelling.

Worse still, a fund with a 3x paper gain and no DPI might look strong on paper, but it has zero flexibility. No capital to return, no leverage for new investments, and no ability to satisfy investors who are, increasingly, asking tough questions.

The Secondary Market Reality Check

One pressure release valve has been the secondary market. Investors can sell their fund interests to other buyers at a discount, or Fund Managers can initiate continuation vehicles that allow existing assets to be rolled into new structures.

But here's the hard truth: secondaries only work if someone else wants the exposure. And right now, many secondary buyers are demanding steep discounts. That $50 million NAV? It might trade at $30 million. Or less.

The rise in secondary activity is a symptom of the larger illness: funds are not exiting quickly enough. Investors are tired of waiting. And if the only option is to sell at a discount, they will, just to clean up their books and redeploy somewhere with clearer timelines.

The Leaky Bucket of Follow-On Rounds

Delayed exits also create a compounding capital drain. Most early-stage companies require follow-on capital. If your exit horizon extends by 2 or 3 years, your fund may have to hold the same portfolio longer than planned. That means holding back reserves, writing additional checks, and reducing dry powder for new opportunities.

And if those follow-ons don't produce outsized results, all you've done is water the losers. This eats into the return profile and raises uncomfortable questions about capital efficiency.

By the end of year ten, many funds look more like triage wards than rocket ships. Capital is tied up in bridge rounds. Exits are frozen. Investors are restless. And the fund manager is running a quiet campaign to explain why everything is still fine.

It's not fine.

In Part 5, we'll close out the chapter by revisiting the fundamental misalignment of incentives between investors and the Venture Capital model, and preview how a multi-asset approach starts to realign those priorities.

Part 5: The Misalignment and the Path Forward

There's a quiet frustration building in the Venture Capital ecosystem, and it's coming from all sides.

Founders feel squeezed. Investors feel stuck. And Fund Managers, many of whom are still charging fees on decade-old funds, are struggling to make sense of a strategy that once felt elegant but now feels archaic.

At the root of all this tension is a fundamental misalignment.

Misalignment Between Time and Return

Venture funds are structured around a timeline that no longer matches the realities of capital deployment, company growth, or liquidity events. Ten-year funds with two-year investment periods were modeled on the assumption that exits would occur in years six through eight. That timeline worked when companies could scale fast and exit faster. It worked when IPOs were frequent, and acquirers were flush with cash.

But today's path to maturity is longer and bumpier. It often takes a company ten years just to become a viable acquisition target. Add in a market downturn or two, and that timeline stretches even further. In the meantime, the venture fund sits, clock ticking, as IRR decays.

Misalignment Between Risk and Reward

Let's not forget that Venture Capital is one of the few asset classes where the providers of capital, the Investors, take on the lion's share of the risk, while the managers, the Fund Managers, are rewarded upfront.

Fund Managers collect management fees regardless of performance. They get carried interest even if only a handful of companies succeed. They rarely suffer consequences if the rest of the portfolio collapses. The asymmetry is built in.

This might be tolerable in a bull market where everyone's getting rich. But in a post-ZIRP environment with rising opportunity costs, Investors are starting to ask why they're underwriting all the downside for theoretical upside they may never see.

Misalignment Between Strategy and Structure

Even the most seasoned VCs are constrained by their fund structures. They may spot great opportunities that don't fit the mold, a cash-flowing business, a growth-stage company that needs structured debt, or a roll-up play better suited for private equity, but their fund documents won't allow it. They're forced to stick to the script. Seed. Series A. Follow-on. Pray for exit.

Meanwhile, more adaptive capital strategies are emerging that can offer funding across the entire capital stack, equity, debt, and hybrid instruments, and are less beholden to binary outcomes.

What Investors Really Want

After dozens of investor meetings, I've come to believe most institutional investors aren't asking for magic. They want three simple things:

- A reasonable return

- A predictable timeline

- A strategy that doesn't rely on the market doing you a favor

They're not asking for 10x unicorns. They're asking for capital that compounds. They want to know that the money they allocate will grow and return in a time frame that makes sense for their own obligations.

If Venture Capital can't deliver that and today, it mostly can't, then capital will migrate elsewhere. And it already is.

The Path Forward

What we need is a strategy that reflects how capital actually works, not how pitch decks pretend it does. That means:

- Flexibility across the capital stack.

- A mix of income and appreciation.

- Structures that allow for early liquidity without sacrificing long-term upside.

- Managers who act like fiduciaries, not just storytellers.

This is where Full-Stack Venture Capital Funds™ begin to show their value. By blending Venture Capital with private credit and private equity, managers can build portfolios that generate income, preserve optionality, and reduce correlation risk. They can back companies in ways that align with each stage of their journey, rather than trying to force every founder into the same Series A-to-IPO funnel.

This stylized illustration provides an illustrative comparison of how the Full-Stack Venture Capital Funds™ model enhances capital flow, job creation, exit outcomes, and community impact compared to the traditional VC model..

TRADITIONAL VC MODEL VS FULL-STACK VENTURE CAPITAL FUND MODEL

A comparison of how capital structures shape local economies, job creation, and community impact.

FULL-STACK VENTURE CAPITAL BDC MODEL

- **Capital Flow:** Capital stays and circulates within local economies, supporting continued growth.

- **Exits:** Exits are managed thoughtfully to ensure ongoing benefits for the community.

- **Job Creation:** Enables long-term job creation, retaining local employment and talent.

- **Community Impact:** Builds infrastructure and amplifies wealth within the local ecosystem.

TRADITIONAL VC MODEL

- **Capital Flow:** Capital flows in and out of local ecosystems, with limited reinvestment.

- **Exits:** Exits often lead to company relocations, reducing local economic benefits.

- **Job Creation:** Jobs are temporary and frequently move elsewhere post-exit.

- **Community Impact:** Minimal long-term contribution to local wealth or infrastructure.

This isn't about abandoning venture capital. It's about maturing it. Evolving it. Making it useful again.

In the next chapter, we'll explore what Full-Stack Venture Capital Funds™ actually look like, how they function, and why they may be the most rational path forward for institutional capital looking to support innovation without being held hostage by outdated structures.

Because the cracks in the capital stack are real, so is the opportunity to rebuild something stronger in its place.

Chapter 2

Why Full-Stack Venture Capital Funds™ Make More Sense Now

Part 1: Defining the Full-Stack Venture Capital Funds™

Let's start with a confession.

When I first heard someone use the term "multi-asset strategy", I assumed it was another branding gimmick. Venture Capitalists have a habit of inventing new phrases to explain old ideas. The same way every slide deck now says "platform," "flywheel," or "ecosystem," the phrase "multi-asset" initially struck me as just another label, like calling yourself a "value-based founder" when your last startup burned $10 million on marketing and WeWork credits.

But then I started living it, managing a family office forces you to think in real-world terms. You're not investing for management fees or paper marks. You're investing to grow and protect actual capital, your own or the capital entrusted to you. And over time, it became undeniable: investing that integrated multiple asset classes, rather than siloing them, performed better, lasted longer, and navigated volatility more effectively.

So, what exactly do we mean when we talk about a Full-Stack Venture Capital Funds™ in the context of venture capital?

Let's start with: "What exactly is a BDC?"

Business Development Companies, or BDCs, were created in the 1980s by Congress to unleash capital into the U.S. economy, specifically into U.S. small- and mid-sized businesses that could not access public markets or secure traditional bank financing.

Think of a BDC as a blend of a venture capital fund, a private credit shop, and a dividend-paying investment trust. It was designed to fund real operating companies, often in the messy, overlooked lower- and middle-market, while providing structure, transparency, and built-in accountability to BDC shareholders.

Unlike traditional private funds, BDCs are regulated investment companies under the Securities and Exchange Commission's 1940 Act and must distribute at least 90 percent of their taxable income to maintain pass-through tax status. That means the BDC itself pays no income tax, and investors receive their share of the income directly, without being taxed twice.

It gets even more compelling for certain investors. Because of how BDCs are structured, those distributions typically do not trigger Unrelated Business Taxable Income, or UBTI. That's a significant advantage for IRAs, trusts, and other tax-sensitive vehicles. The result is clean income, passed through efficiently and predictably, without the unpleasant surprises often associated with LP interests in traditional private equity or venture capital funds.

BDCs also offer a structural feature most other traditional venture capital and private equity funds cannot access. They are legally allowed to use up to two-to-one leverage on their Net Asset Value (NAV). When used prudently, this leverage can amplify returns and accelerate net asset growth in a way traditional fund structures rarely can. It is not about loading up on risky debt. It is about using well-secured credit to support more companies and generate consistent income across the portfolio.

Many traditional venture capital and private equity funds avoid the BDC structure because of the regulatory complexity. The compliance burden, public reporting requirements, and ongoing disclosures are more than most fund managers are willing to take on. It is not as easy and certainly not as discreet.

But for the few of us who are willing to embrace the model, the BDC offers a different kind of opportunity. It is transparent. It is durable. And it is deeply aligned with the people it is meant to serve. Founders gain access to more versatile capital. Investors receive income along the way. And communities benefit from companies that are built to last rather than built to exit.

In the context of this book, and as an investment model, the BDC is not just a regulatory wrapper. It is a delivery system for a full-stack ventures capital fund. It allows funds to combine venture equity, private credit, and growth-stage buyouts within a single strategy. It supports long-term alignment and sustainable outcomes. And most important, it creates a new way to think about investing across the full arc of a company's growth.

It is not for every manager or every strategy. But for those who believe in building something more complete, the BDC structure might be one of the most elegant solutions available.

The Full-Stack Venture Capital Funds™

Likewise, this is not just a fund with a wide mandate. It's not a VC firm that occasionally dabbles in private credit. It's a structurally integrated model that deliberately combines three elements of private market investing:

- Venture Capital – For early-stage equity, innovation exposure, and high-upside bets

- Private Credit – For steady income, downside protection, and capital structure control

- Private Equity or Growth Buyouts – For long-term ownership, compounding enterprise value, and operational leverage

Together, these form the backbone of a strategy that is not only diversified across return types but diversified across timelines, risk profiles, exit paths, and capital efficiency levers.

THE RISE OF THE MULTI-ASSET ARCHETYPE

A visual overview of the four essential components, Early-Stage Equity, Private Credit, Growth Buyouts, and Revenue Participation/Dividends, that together form the Full-Stack Venture Capital Funds™ model.

This isn't about throwing darts at three different boards. It's about building a single portfolio that uses the right tool for each company, each investment, and each moment in the capital cycle. It's capital that adapts.

Why the VC-Only Model Falls Short

Traditional Venture Capital relies almost entirely on equity. It assumes that ownership is the primary lever of value. You buy early, hold long, and hope for exponential growth. In a perfect world, you exit through IPO or acquisition, realize a massive gain, and look like a genius.

But in the real world, companies evolve unevenly. Markets shift. Teams stumble. Not every great product becomes a great business. And not every business needs equity capital at every stage.

Sometimes what a company needs is a line of credit, not another priced round.

Sometimes what a founder needs is a growth buyout, not more dilution.

Sometimes the best way to return value is through income, not just long-term paper appreciation.

The Full-Stack Venture Capital Funds™ solves for this. It lets you meet companies where they are, not where your fund structure needs them to be.

A Portfolio Designed for Real Life

Imagine this portfolio construction:

- A seed-stage medical device startup receives a small equity investment with follow-on potential.

- A Series B software company receives a revenue-based loan structured around monthly recurring revenue.

- A profitable manufacturing firm raises growth capital through a preferred equity buyout with downside protection.

- A consumer brand with distribution traction receives working capital debt to finance inventory for Q4 holiday sales.

- A post-accelerator hardware startup is funded with a convertible note paired with warrant coverage, giving equity optionality and near-term protection.

This isn't five different funds. This is one fund designed to operate across the spectrum of needs, risks, and return profiles. And it isn't some untested dream. It's already being done.

In the next section, we'll explore how combining equity, debt, and growth buyouts within a single vehicle actually creates more resilience, especially during volatile markets and tightening liquidity cycles.

Part 2: How Combining Equity, Debt, and Growth Buyouts Creates Resilience

If you've spent enough time around startup investing, you'll eventually hear some version of this phrase: "We're not bankers. We take real risks." It's usually said with pride, maybe even a little swagger, as if debt is somehow beneath venture capital's creative daring.

But here's the irony. Most of the iconic companies in the modern tech landscape, from Apple to Amazon to Tesla, used debt as a growth tool, not as a last resort, but as a disciplined accelerator. It gave them runway. It preserved ownership. It forced them to act like real businesses.

What makes the Full-Stack Venture Capital Funds™ model powerful isn't just the ability to write checks in different formats. It's the ability to withstand market cycles, portfolio turbulence, and funding delays without leaning solely on hope and follow-ons. In a venture-only portfolio, everything rides on high-risk equity. In a Full-Stack Venture Capital Funds™ portfolio, you have multiple ways to win and multiple ways to protect yourself if or when the winds shift.

Equity Is the Upside Engine

Let's be clear. Equity is still essential. It's the only way to participate in the exponential upside that innovation sometimes produces. A cap table position in a breakout company, acquired or IPO'd at the right time, is transformative. It's what makes Venture Capital exciting in the first place.

But it's also unpredictable. Equity, by nature, absorbs all the risk. If the company falters, pivots, or dies slowly on the vine, equity holders typically get wiped out.

That's where the other pieces come in.

Debt Is the Stability Layer

Private credit, structured correctly, offers predictable returns. Interest payments begin immediately. The investor has defined covenants, often with collateral, a superior position in the capital stack, and equity kickers in the form of warrants and options. While venture debt is sometimes used poorly as a bridge to nowhere when aligned with a revenue-generating business or tied to debt service coverage minimums and performance milestones, it can be an elegant instrument.

Let's say a company has $3 million in annual recurring revenue and healthy gross margins. Instead of raising more equity and further diluting the founders and early investors, they borrow $1 million at a reasonable rate. The money gets used for sales hires or inventory expansion. Growth accelerates. Cash flow improves. Everyone wins.

And the fund benefits from yield real cash returns, not just paper marks.

In a venture-only portfolio, there is no yield. It's binary. But in a Full-Stack Venture Capital Funds™ portfolio, private credit generates ballast. That income helps smooth out performance across the fund. When one equity position stumbles, the debt side of the portfolio keeps paying.

Growth Buyouts Add Long-Term Durability

Likewise, private equity has long understood something that venture funds often forget: control creates value. Buying into a growth-stage company, installing operational support, aligning incentives, and growing enterprise value over time is not as flashy as chasing unicorns, but it often produces better outcomes.

In a Full-Stack Venture Capital Funds™, growth buyouts create anchor investments. These are companies that are already generating EBITDA. Traditional PE firms may overlook them because they're too small or too messy. But with the right capital and oversight, they scale beautifully.

Imagine owning 60 percent of a regional healthcare provider that's profitable and expanding. You help finance a new clinic, improve billing systems, and introduce tech-enabled efficiencies. After three years, the business doubles, and you exit to a strategic buyer, a sponsor, or even through an ESOP.

That outcome may not make headlines. But it produces real cash-on-cash returns, which help de-risk the rest of the fund.

A Portfolio That Bends, Not Breaks

Here's the real advantage. When markets tighten, exits slow, or valuations compress, a single-asset venture fund has almost no flexibility. They either keep funding their companies or let them die. There's no middle ground.

A Full-Stack Venture Capital Funds™, by contrast, can reallocate. It can shift toward credit during turbulent cycles. It can support portfolio companies with non-dilutive capital. It can exit one buyout while continuing to hold an equity position in another company that needs time.

This optionality isn't just convenient, it's strategic. It means the fund can adapt without panicking. And that, more than anything, is the hallmark of resilience.

In Part 3, we'll explore how this adaptability plays out on the ground, specifically how Full-Stack Venture Capital Funds™ are able to meet the full spectrum of a startup's capital needs, from pre-seed vision to profitable expansion.

Part 3: Meeting the Full Spectrum of a Startup's Capital Needs

Founders don't wake up thinking, "I need a Series B." They think, "I need $3 million to build this feature, expand my sales team, or open a second location." The label seed, Series A, mezzanine, bridge is an invention of finance people. What companies actually need is capital that aligns with their stage, trajectory, and risk profile.

Here's the problem with traditional VC: it only knows how to deliver one flavor of money, equity. It's like showing up to every dinner party with a bottle of red wine. Sometimes that's perfect. Sometimes the host is serving oysters.

What startups need and what multi-asset funds can provide is a full menu. Not just capital, but capital that's *fit for purpose*.

The Early Stage: When Vision Outruns Revenue

At the earliest stages, capital is pure belief. There's often no product, no revenue, and sometimes no team, just a founder, a deck, and a dream. This is where equity makes the most sense. The risk is astronomical, but so is the potential upside.

Still, even here, there's room for creativity. SAFE notes and convertible debt have become standard tools because they delay valuation discussions and create flexibility. A Full-Stack Venture Capital Funds™ with credit expertise can write these instruments with more precision, tying them to milestones, protecting downside, and aligning terms with future institutional rounds.

And more importantly, these early investments don't need to sit idle. The same fund might provide light working capital debt to help the company get its MVP across the finish line. Or, better yet, fund the *customer* of the startup a clever form of demand-side capital that's rarely seen in pure VC.

The Growth Stage: When Momentum Needs Fuel

Let's say the company has traction. Revenue's growing, customers are sticky, and unit economics are decent. The founder faces a familiar dilemma: raise more equity and dilute, or try to bootstrap and risk missing the moment.

This is the "messy middle" where many startups stall, not because they aren't good businesses, but because their funding options are limited.

Full-Stack Venture Capital Funds™ shines here. They can offer structured credit to extend runway, growth equity to capture a larger market, or a partial buyout to provide founder liquidity without derailing momentum. These aren't exotic moves, they're just uncommon in venture.

A founder who owns 60% of their company and wants to de-risk without losing control? A Full-Stack Venture Capital Funds™ can buy 20%, offer a $1 million term loan, and become a partner in scaling, not just an observer with pro rata rights.

The Expansion Stage: When Scale Demands Infrastructure

Scaling a company is like moving from a rowboat to a cargo ship. The founder needs capital for talent, systems, expansion, maybe even M&A. This is where traditional VC often tap out. Either they lack the capital for a major round, or they hand the baton to growth equity firms or non-bank lenders who really don't know the founder and don't care about their journey.

A Full-Stack Venture Capital Funds™ can follow through. It can provide mezzanine loans to push next funding rounds further downstream at even higher valuations, and then syndicate or even lead the next round. It can also underwrite strategic acquisitions or fund the buildout of physical infrastructure through credit. This long arc of capital alignment builds trust, and that trust creates better outcomes.

And because the fund holds both credit and equity positions, it has more insight into real-time performance. It's not waiting for quarterly board updates. It's in the weeds, helping to navigate.

The Maturity Stage: When Exit Isn't the Only Option

Here's a secret: not every company needs to exit. Some companies can become profitable, growing machines that throw off cash for years. But Venture Capital, with its fund cycle and return profile, *needs* exits. That's the only way it gets paid.

Full-Stack Venture Capital Funds™ isn't so rigid. If a company reaches maturity, the fund can recapitalize it, take dividends, or prepare it for a patient exit rather than a fire sale. And because the fund has PE and credit capabilities, it can even sponsor a management buyout or bring in strategic operators without pushing the founder to the curb.

This flexibility is liberating. It creates more paths to success, not fewer. And for founders who've poured their lives into a company, that optionality is worth more than any term sheet.

Capital as a Continuum, Not a Transaction

What all of this boils down to is a philosophical shift. Instead of thinking of capital as a sequence of disconnected rounds, the Full-Stack Venture Capital Funds™ treats capital as a continuum, a strategic resource that evolves alongside the company.

This doesn't just serve founders better. It also gives investors more data, better relationships, and the ability to compound returns over time. Instead of exiting at Series C and watching from the sidelines, the fund can participate in the full journey.

In Part 4, we'll explore how this full-spectrum approach leads to broader capital efficiency not just for the companies, but for the fund managers themselves.

Part 4: Broader Capital Efficiency for Portfolio Companies and Fund Managers

Capital efficiency isn't just a finance buzzword. It's a survival skill.

If the last decade taught us anything, it's that throwing money at startups doesn't guarantee success. For every unicorn that scaled efficiently, there are a dozen others that raised nine-figure rounds, installed two espresso machines in the office, hired a TikTok strategist, and still couldn't find product-market fit.

And from the fund manager's seat, the problem is just as bad. Dollars go out the door fast. They come back slow. If they even come back at all. This is not a game for the impatient or undercapitalized. Unless, of course, you change the rules.

That's where Full-Stack Venture Capital Funds™ strategies come in. They aren't just better for startups. They're better for the stewards of capital, too.

Let's Start with the Startups

A capital-efficient company is one that gets more output from every dollar of input, but that doesn't happen by accident. It happens when the capital matches the need.

Here's a simple example. A company has a recurring revenue stream of $150,000 per month, strong customer retention, and a high-margin product. They want to invest in onboarding automation to reduce churn and unlock scale. They don't need a $10 million equity round. They need $1.5 million in growth capital and maybe some operational support.

Traditional VC says, "Raise a Series B and let's double your valuation." The founder hands over another 20 percent of the company and now has new investors breathing down their neck for a 10x outcome.

A Full-Stack Venture Capital Funds™ looks at the same business and says, "We can provide a structured revenue-based credit line to fund this specific need. No dilution for you as founder. If it works, we can revisit an equity infusion later. If it doesn't, you haven't lost your shirt." Guess what? That seems like such a nice gesture, but the Full-Stack Venture Capital Funds™ also doesn't get diluted by that same 20%.

The founder keeps control. The company grows into the capital. The investors see cash flows sooner. Everyone sleeps better.

Now Let's Talk About the Fund Managers

Traditional VC fund managers operate like trapeze artists. They leap from raise to raise, hoping their timing aligns with a good exit or a hot markup.

The issue is timing. A fund manager calls 100 percent of capital early, spends the next three years deploying it, and then sits tight for the next seven, hoping the IPO window opens or M&A heats up. Returns take a decade. Liquidity takes longer. And God help them if they need to raise Fund III before Fund I has distributed anything but slide decks and sizzle reels.

Full-Stack Venture Capital Funds™ managers? They have tools. More importantly, they have cash flows.

Credit investments generate interest payments. PE transactions can generate dividends or partial exits. These interim cash flows allow the fund to recycle capital, reduce dependence on the exit gods, and demonstrate traction to Investors in quarters, not decades.

This model also aligns better with today's institutional LP base. Endowments, pensions, and family offices are sophisticated. They want yield. They want optionality. And they want exposure to innovation without underwriting binary outcomes on a five-year timer.

Recycling Capital Means Recycling Opportunity

When capital comes back early, it can be redeployed. Not just to the next hot startup, but to the same founder, now solving the next problem.

Instead of one and done, Full-Stack Venture Capital Funds™ can follow the full arc of a founder's capital stack. Start with a seed check, layer in a line of credit when traction hits. Participate in a growth equity round. Back their bolt-on acquisition. This flywheel of familiarity and trust creates a competitive edge.

It also lowers friction. A founder who has to explain their entire business model to every new investor at every stage wastes precious time. With a Full-Stack Venture Capital Funds™ as their Capital Partner, the conversation evolves. It doesn't restart.

Let's Talk About Volatility

Every asset class has cycles, but they don't move in lockstep.

When venture is cold, credit might be hot. When public markets are shaky, private equity can pick up assets at a discount. This uncorrelated motion gives Full-Stack Venture Capital Funds™ internal ballast.

Instead of selling at the wrong time or chasing returns into froth, they can allocate tactically. Preserve gains. Capture upside. And stay disciplined.

In a world where macroeconomic shocks come in 18-month intervals, that's not just an advantage. It's a necessity!

What About the Critics?

There are purists who argue that focus is a virtue. That blending of strategies makes you a generalist, not a jack of all trades who is master of none.

To that I say: Have you seen the VC returns lately?

The reality is that capital formation needs to evolve. It's not about doing everything. It's about doing what works. If your fund can underwrite risk across the spectrum, why wouldn't you?

Besides, most venture firms already make accidental credit investments. They just don't call them that. Every time they fund a money-losing company with no clear path to exit, they're giving away equity and hoping it doesn't turn into a zero-coupon, non-performing bond.

At least Full-Stack Venture Capital Funds™ are honest about it.

Putting It All Together

Capital efficiency isn't a tactic. It's a worldview.

It means giving founders what they need, when they need it, in a form that makes sense. It means managing portfolios for total return, not just paper gains. And it means acknowledging that in a complex world, flexibility beats purity every time.

We're not trying to reinvent Venture Capital. We're trying to improve it. Make it faster. Smarter. More human.

And that starts with thinking beyond a single type of check.

PORTFOLIO CONSTRUCTION FOR OPTIONALITY

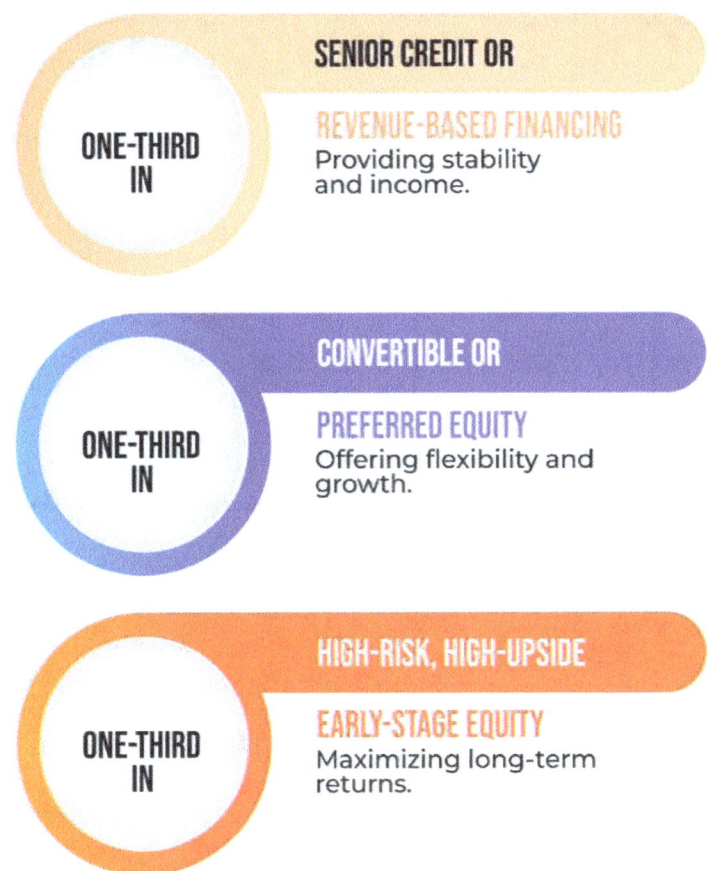

Portfolio Construction for Optionality in a Full-Stack Venture Capital Funds™.

Chapter 3

The Structural Shift Toward Total Return

Part 1: Income + Appreciation Models vs. Long-Only Growth

There was a time I thought "total return" was something only bond guys cared about. Back then, I was still drinking the Kool-Aid or maybe the kombucha of long-only venture growth. All that mattered was the J-curve. Just wait, they'd say. The value will come. Sit tight, ignore the lack of distributions, and think of all the paper wealth we've created.

Except that paper wealth doesn't pay college tuition. Or payroll. Or the mortgage on the second home bought when rates were still under three percent. Sorry to go off topic...

What I eventually realized and what this chapter unpacks is that the traditional long-only growth model in Venture Capital is no longer sufficient. Not because it never worked, but because it doesn't work anymore. Not in this market, at this scale, or for this generation of founders and VC funders.

Total return isn't just a different way of calculating success. It's fundamentally different in how it's built.

The Seduction of Growth-Only Thinking

Let's call it what it is. Growth-only investing is a hell of a drug.

You invest early. You watch the valuation double, then triple, and suddenly you're calculating IRRs in your head during board meetings. But it's all theoretical until there's a real liquidity event. And those are fewer and farther between these days.

TOTAL RETURN VS. GROWTH-ONLY MODELS

KEY DIFFERENCES:

ASPECT	GROWTH-ONLY MODEL	TOTAL RETURN MODEL (FULL-STACK BDC)
Return Strategy	Focused on growth, relying on exits	Combines income generation (interest, dividends) and capital appreciation.
Risk Management	High risk with no immediate returns	Mitigates risk with early cash flow from structured debt and equity, and diversification.
Capital Efficiency	Bet on a few big wins, often requiring high equity stakes and time.	Diversified and flexible returns from a mix of structured credit, early cash flow, and equity growth.
Founder Impact	Focused on dilution; founders must give up significant equity.	Flexible capital solutions, including non-dilutive debt and royalties, reducing dilution.

Key differences between Growth-Only Venture Models and Total Return Models, highlighting the shift toward structured, diversified, and income-supported return strategies

The promise of long-only growth rests on three assumptions:

- There will be consistent access to follow-on capital.

- Valuations will rise predictably over time.

- There will be robust exit opportunities, whether IPO or M&A, within a decade.

All three are increasingly suspect.

Today, capital markets are twitchy. Strategic acquirers are pickier. IPOs are the investment banking equivalent of finding a parking spot in Manhattan, technically possible, but rarely convenient and almost always overpriced.

So, what happens? Startups keep raising. Dilution stacks up. Fund timelines get pushed. And when liquidity finally arrives, it limps in, underwhelming and overdue.

The Case for Income Plus Appreciation

Enter the Full-Stack Venture Capital Funds™ model. It's not a fancy rebrand. It's a smarter foundation.

At its core, total return combines income realized cash flows during the life of the investment and appreciation, meaning long-term equity value realized at exit. It borrows from the private equity and credit playbooks and fuses them with the upside profile of VC.

This model treats every dollar as a working asset. Not a bet to be locked away until the exit gods smile. If you can generate yield and build enterprise value at the same time, why wouldn't you?

Picture this:

- You invest in a company with a strong cash flow profile.

- Instead of taking only equity, you blend in structured credit.

- You earn quarterly interest payments or royalties.

- As the company grows, you convert warrants or preferred equity into long-term gains.

You're earning while you wait. You've bought time. And, more importantly, you've created options.

Founders Like It Too

Founders, for their part, are waking up to this shift. Not every entrepreneur wants to blitzscale. Not everyone wants to go public. Many want to build sustainable, valuable companies that generate profits and create outcomes.

When you offer a founder a term sheet that includes non-dilutive capital alongside strategic equity, they don't see that as conservative. They see it as responsible, especially after watching peers raise monster rounds only to lay off half the staff two quarters later.

The old VC pitch was "Give us 25 percent of your company now, and we'll help you raise more later." The new pitch, "our pitch," is: "Let's give you the right capital at the right time, so you keep control and still have room to grow."

It's not a trade-off between innovation and discipline. It's the new definition of both.

Building Portfolios That Can Breathe

One of the biggest problems with long-only growth portfolios is their binary nature. The model essentially assumes most companies will fail, and a few will carry the fund.

In contrast, Full-Stack Venture Capital Funds™ portfolios are designed to function in more scenarios.

Some companies generate steady income and modest growth.

Others hit big exits.

Some underperform but still return capital through structured deals.

You're no longer betting the farm on one or two outliers. You're building a more diverse, more resilient, and more functional portfolio.

You also de-risk the capital base. Investors begin receiving returns earlier. Fund managers have proof of performance to raise future funds. Founders get more control. And the whole ecosystem moves from promise to performance.

What Wall Street Already Knows

Look at REITs. Look at closed-end funds. Look at interval funds. These vehicles have long embraced total return principles, blending income with capital gains to create smoother return profiles.

Yet in Venture Capital, we act like the only way to win is to hold our breath for a decade and hope for a home run.

Even traditional PE firms are adapting. They've long captured cash flows through dividends and recapitalizations. Now, many are offering structured equity deals and hybrid credit structures, especially in the lower-middle market.

Why? Because predictability matters. Especially in environments where volatility is high and capital is no longer cheap.

Your Investors Want This

Let's be blunt. Institutional investors are tired of waiting. Tired of markdowns. Tired of updates that talk about "strong pipeline visibility" while distributions remain stuck at zero.

They want yield. They want upside. They want both.

A Full-Stack Venture Capital Funds™ model doesn't just serve them better, it speaks their language. It creates visibility, demonstrates discipline, and builds real financial architecture around the venture asset class.

When you show an investor that your fund is generating income and still has upside in the tank, you're not pitching hope. You're showing proof.

Closing Out the First Mile

We'll dive deeper into the other components of total return in the next sections capital recycling, payback periods, and avoiding binary outcomes, but it starts here: replacing the VC fantasy of a singular big bang with a more layered, more flexible, and ultimately more profitable reality.

In this world, returns aren't just backloaded. They're sequenced. Modeled. Managed. Earned.

This is the new math of innovation capital.

Part 2: Avoiding Vintage Risk and Capital Recycling Constraints

Ask any experienced vintner cultivating grapes and they'll tell you: no two harvest strategies are the same. In private markets, we have our own version of that variability, and we call it "vintage risk." It's the danger of committing capital into a particular economic window only to discover, years later, that the window came with a broken hinge.

In traditional Venture Capital, where funds are raised in fixed cycles, typically every three to four years this risk is baked into the cake. You raise a fund, deploy it over a 2- to 4-year window, and then pray that market conditions, exits, and multiples cooperate. If your deployment coincided with 2021? You were buying growth-stage companies at preposterous valuations. If you waited until 2023? You found yourself backing founders who had just survived the reset and were leaner, hungrier, and a lot more realistic.

STAGE 1 — GROWTH PHASE WITHOUT PROFITABILITY

Company is growing but not yet profitable, requiring capital to reach the next growth milestone.

STAGE 2 — TRADITIONAL EQUITY IN EXCESSIVE DILUTION

The company attempts to raise equity, but this leads to high dilution for the founders and early investors.

STAGE 3 — COMPANY SECURES STRUCTURED CREDIT

Instead of equity, the company takes on structured credit to extend runway without diluting ownership.

STAGE 4 — ACHIEVING GROWTH MILESTONES

With the capital secured, the company hits growth milestones, improving its financials, customer metrics, and valuation.

STAGE 5 — NEW EQUITY RAISE FROM A POSITION OF STRENGTH

The company is now able to raise equity at a higher valuation, reducing the dilution and improving the outcome for investors.

Multi-Stage Capital Efficiency Pathway , illustrating how companies move from early unprofitable growth through structured credit, efficiency milestones, and into stronger, higher-valuation equity raises.

Now imagine if, instead of playing roulette with macro timing, you could build a strategy that insulates against the randomness of vintage cycles. That's where Full-Stack Venture Capital Funds™'s total-return-focused models begin to shine.

The Problem with the Fixed Fund Lifecycle

Let's start with the elephant in the data room. Venture Capital fund cycles are rigid.

You raise, you deploy, you harvest. Rinse and repeat.

But this rigidity assumes:

- You'll always find great companies when your fund is "on"

- You'll always have dry powder when markets dislocate.

- The capital you return will be enough to raise your next fund.

That's a nice story. But reality doesn't work on a tidy calendar. Great investments don't arrive on schedule, and the best deals often emerge during chaos, not calm.

When your capital is locked in a drawdown structure with rigid timelines, you're either sitting on dry powder with nothing worth funding, or you're out of cash when opportunities are screaming for attention.

Even worse, when companies need more time or more capital, you're stuck between overextending the fund's life or telling your Investors the dreaded phrase: "we're doing a bridge round."

Why Recycling Capital Isn't as Easy as It Sounds

Let's say you're lucky enough to have a few early exits or realizations in a traditional fund. You'd think recycling that capital into new opportunities would be simple. But no compliance, LP agreements, and fund covenants can make it painfully difficult.

Most LPAs (Limited Partnership Agreements) set tight restrictions on how much capital can be recycled. Often, there's a ceiling of 25-30% for commitments. And even then, you have to declare intent, track it meticulously, and sometimes seek approvals. By the time you've navigated the paperwork, the opportunity is gone.

This makes traditional VC funds inflexible and sluggish just when nimbleness would deliver the highest returns.

A Better Approach: Capital that Flows, Not Sits

In a Full-Stack Venture Capital Funds™ model, capital isn't treated like museum art locked away until some gala event. It flows. It moves between debt, equity, and structured positions depending on need and return profile.

Let's say you fund a company through a convertible note or revenue-based financing structure. It starts paying interest or royalties in the second year. You now have real cash flow coming back to the fund, not paper gains.

With that cash, you can do a few things:

- Reinvest in the next deal.

- Support an existing portfolio company.

- Build reserves for opportunistic market timing.

You're no longer beholden to the drawdown cycle. You've decoupled the engine of your returns from the calendar.

That's not just more efficient, it's more survivable.

Vintage Diversification Through Multi-Asset Exposure

A Full-Stack Venture Capital Funds™ strategy doesn't just let you move capital faster. It allows you to invest across multiple economic conditions.

Private credit, for example, performs well in rising-rate environments and in uncertain macro conditions. Venture Capital shines during bull markets or innovation booms. Private equity and control buyouts offer downside protection through operational influence and structured governance.

If you're running a fund with exposure to all three, your capital isn't locked into a single bet on a single economy. You're playing across the field. If venture multiples compress, your credit deals are still generating yield. If credit markets freeze, you lean into equity or hybrid deals where you control outcomes.

This is how you build vintage diversification: not by time-stamping your deals, but by asset-class blending.

The Reserves Fallacy

Here's another dirty little secret in the traditional VC world: reserves are a trap.

Most Venture Capital funds set aside 50% or more of their committed capital for follow-ons. In theory, this ensures you can support your winners. In practice, it's a guessing game.

Sometimes you over-allocate to underperformers out of loyalty. Other times, you under-support your best companies because the reserve math didn't anticipate their true capital needs.

This creates a paradox: you hold onto capital out of caution, which limits new deal flow, but then still struggle when your best companies need larger checks.

Full-Stack Venture Capital Funds™ models don't need traditional reserves. They use cash flow and debt repayments to dynamically fund follow-ons. You're not choosing between supporting winners and finding new ones; you're doing both, in real time, with real liquidity.

Better Fund Math, Better Behavior

There's also a behavioral benefit to avoiding vintage constraints. Fund managers are human. When a fund nears the end of its investment period, there's pressure to "put money to work." That leads to rushed decisions, marginal deals, and a distortion of the fund's original strategy.

Worse, when the end-of-fund-life looms, Fund Managers often prioritize internal rate of return (IRR) games over long-term company outcomes. We've all seen it: rushed exits to goose metrics before the next fundraising cycle.

When your capital is evergreen or recycled efficiently, you can resist that pressure. You can wait. You can be deliberate.

And most importantly, you can act like an investor instead of a bureaucrat trapped in a vest.

The Investor Perspective: Smoother, More Predictable Returns

For Investors, capital flexibility means more than better returns; it means better planning.

Institutional Investors have allocation targets, cash flow modeling, and liquidity schedules to manage. Traditional VC funds throw wrenches into all of that. Capital gets called sporadically, returns trickle in unpredictably, and NAVs become abstract art during down cycles.

In contrast, a fund that generates income and recycles capital provides:

- More consistent distributions.

- Easier reallocation planning.

- Lower cash drag on uncalled capital.

This isn't just better math. It's a better investor experience.

Letting Markets Be Your Ally

A final note on timing. When your fund can recycle capital or reinvest dynamically, you're no longer fighting the market; you're working with it.

Let's say the IPO window reopens and valuations skyrocket for six months. You can lean into equity and capture upside. Then rates rise and equity cools. You shift back to private credit and structured deals that deliver income.

This is what public market investors call tactical allocation. In the private world, it's just called common sense.

But you can only do it if your capital strategy is built to flex, not freeze.

Part 3: Shorter Payback Periods and Optionality in Exits

Venture Capital has always had a romance problem. We fall hard and fast for startups with a grand vision, and then we wait. And wait. And wait some more. It's like being in a relationship where you've moved in, met the parents, and still don't know if there's ever going to be a wedding or worse, a breakup. The capital is committed. The hope is strong. But the return? "Pending."

This wouldn't be such a problem if waiting didn't come with opportunity cost. Traditional VC asks Investors to accept a zero cash return for 5, 7, and sometimes even 10 years. For many institutional investors, this creates real pressure. Pensions and endowments have liabilities to match. Family offices must consider generational planning. Well, individuals eventually like to see their money again.

So, what if we stopped treating exits as single moments in time and started thinking about capital recovery as a continuum?

The Myth of the Big Bang Exit

Let's bust a myth that plagues most traditional funds: the idea that success only arrives in the form of an IPO or massive acquisition. The term "exit" itself is misleading. It implies a single event, a binary moment. You're in or you're out.

That's not how real value creation works. In fact, many of the best businesses don't "exit" in the traditional sense; they compound. They grow, acquire, reinvest, and spin off cash for decades. But if you're in a fund that only makes money on an IPO, you're forced to push for that outcome even when it may not be the right move. Worse, companies often exit too early to appease their cap table. That's not alignment. That's misaligned desperation.

Revenue Participation and Early Cash Flow

Enter the magic of structured instruments: revenue-based financing, dividend recapitalizations, and other hybrid tools that let you earn while you wait. If you're in a revenue-sharing agreement, for instance, you start getting paid as soon as the business is generating cash, not seven years from now.

That's a game-changer for fund construction. It introduces real yield into what used to be a hope-and-hold model. It also creates more alignment between the investor and the founder. When you're sharing in the success as it happens, instead of just betting on a terminal event, you build a healthier relationship.

Founders love this too. They're no longer pushed to raise again, sell early, or sacrifice mission for milestones. They can build companies with resilience, not just with pitch decks.

Partial Liquidity and Secondary Pathways

Another underutilized strategy in traditional VC: structured secondary sales. Suppose a portfolio company is doing well but needs more time. In that case, there's often a secondary market available either through growth equity funds, strategic partners, or even inside rounds with new terms.

Yet, because most VCs don't want to mark down or complicate cap table math, they avoid these routes. In a Full-Stack Venture Capital Funds™, partial exits are part of the design. You don't need every company to go public. You need a few to pay you back early, a few to cash flow over time, and a few to deliver multiples on longer-term bets.

This layered approach creates a much healthier profile for both IRR and actual distributions through return stacking.

Time to Breakeven Matters More Than Time to Exit

Here's a little-known truth: you can have a stellar IRR and still be underwater in real dollars if your exits are back-weighted and paper-based. Investors don't spend on IRR.

They spend distributions. And every year they go without real cash back is a year of opportunity cost.

This is why the time to breakeven, the moment when an investor has received their original capital back, should matter more than the splashy final exit.

Full-Stack Venture Capital Funds™ strategies let you engineer for earlier breakevens by layering in interest, repayments, and shorter-duration deals. Think about it this way:

- A credit deal may be repaid fully in 2 years.

- A growth equity position might return capital in 4 to 6 years through dividends or recap.

- A venture deal could take 8 to 10 years, but be fully carried by prior cash flows.

This laddered repayment structure smooths out returns and builds investor trust. It's not about de-risking innovation. It's about de-risking the waiting.

The Emotional Side of Optionality

Let's talk about the morale imparitive. In every fund, there comes a moment, usually in years 4 or 5, when you look at the portfolio and realize that the timeline has drifted. Maybe there were delays in product-market fit. Maybe the exit market cooled. Maybe the unicorn you backed just got dehorned.

In traditional VC, there's not much you can do. You ride it out, explain it to Investors, and hope the next update includes a acquisition term sheet.

But in a Full-Stack Venture Capital Funds™ model, you have optionality. Optionality is emotional as much as financial. It means you can provide Investors with liquidity when needed. It means you can pivot from equity to credit if a company needs a bridge instead of a buyout. It means your team feels less pressure to force narratives just to show progress.

Optionality buys patience. And in investing, patience backed by structure is a winning formula.

Multiple Pathways to Realization

Here's what this looks like in action:

- A healthcare SaaS company pays revenue share for 3 years, then is sold to a PE firm.

- A hardware startup repays a note, then issues equity to new investors.

- A consumer brand is recapitalized at Series C, providing partial liquidity via preferred redemption.

- A fintech exits through acquisition after 7 years, with early payouts reducing exposure.

All four scenarios return capital to the fund at different times, through different methods, and without relying on a single IPO.

This isn't theoretical. This is already happening in funds that choose to build flexibly. In fact, it's often the firms using "old" tools like debt and revenue finance that are making the most progress with "new" outcomes.

Exit-Agnostic Investing

The holy grail in this approach is becoming exit-agnostic. Not apathetic, not lazy, just agnostic to the method and timeline.

When your capital structure can flex to meet the company's needs and your own fund's obligations, you free yourself from the tyranny of singular outcomes. You're no longer praying for the one big win. You're building a system of wins, some small, some large, some steady.

This kind of investing is built for durability. It's what allows you to back the next great founder who doesn't want to sell in five years, because she believes she's building a 50-year company. And you can say yes because you'll still get paid along the way.

Part 4: Creating Value Without Overexposure to Binary Outcomes

There's an old saying in Silicon Valley that "you only need one." One massive exit, one decacorn, one IPO that defies gravity, and everything else in the portfolio is forgiven. Losses are expected. Failures are baked in. That one win pays for it all.

But that kind of math assumes a risk appetite and time horizon that's increasingly out of step with today's investors. More importantly, it assumes that capital is an all-or-nothing game. Win big or lose gracefully. Spray and pray.

That's not investing. That's gambling dressed in Patagonia.

The Tyranny of Binary Thinking

Traditional venture has long relied on binary thinking: either a company wins or it fails. But binary outcomes have binary consequences. You're either a genius or a ghost. You get a write-up or a write-off.

This all-or-nothing framework turns fund construction into a numbers game. Build a large enough portfolio and hope one or two carry the load. That's fine in theory. But it's inefficient, capital-intensive, and increasingly misaligned with founders who don't want to live on a roulette wheel.

It's also brutal for Investors, who have to squint through layers of "adjusted" performance metrics to understand whether their money is working or just waiting.

Moving Beyond the Home Run Model

The baseball metaphors in venture are endless. You've got your singles, doubles, triples, and the ever-elusive home run.

But the model is built to swing for the fences. Nobody gets carried at a partner meeting for a solid double. Unless that double returned early capital and provides compounding returns.

In Full-Stack Venture Capital Funds™ strategies, we stop asking every company to be a home run. Some can be singles with interest. Some can be doubles with dividends. Some may never leave the infield, but they don't strike out either.

When you stop needing every company to be a unicorn, you allow founders to build rationally. You allow capital to behave like capital, not like lottery tickets. And you open the door to a different kind of value creation.

Operational Value vs. Exit Value

One of the most powerful shifts in Full-Stack Venture Capital Funds™ investing is moving from "exit value" to "operational value."

Exit value is what the company might be worth to someone else one day. Operational value is what it's worth today based on real metrics. Revenue. Margins. Customer retention. Net cash flow.

When you anchor your investment thesis in operational value, you stop playing the greater-fool game. You stop relying on the next round or the next buyer to validate your position. You can underwrite returns based on business fundamentals, not narrative.

This also means you can help founders in ways that don't just inflate the valuation. You can assist with margin improvement, financing strategy, and go-to-market optimization. You become a partner in performance, not just paper.

Risk Mitigation as a Growth Lever

Here's a secret: reducing risk doesn't reduce return. In fact, in Full-Stack Venture Capital Funds™ models, risk mitigation can amplify returns by keeping companies alive long enough to reach inflection points.

- Structured downside protection keeps early investors from being washed out in later rounds.

- Credit overlays provide bridge capital without valuation distortion.

- Preferred equity and royalties offer intermediate return pathways.

These tools reduce the probability of total loss while preserving upside. That's not conservative. That's intelligent capital design.

Think of it like mountain climbing. You don't reach the summit faster by skipping safety ropes. You reach it by planning the route, managing risk, and pacing your ascent.

Real Optionality Creates Real Value

Most venture capitalists talk about optionality in theory. In practice, they're trapped by their fund's structure. They can't do credit. They can't do minority recaps. They can't hold past 10 years. They're boxed in.

CROSS-ASSET UNDERWRITING AND GOVERNANCE

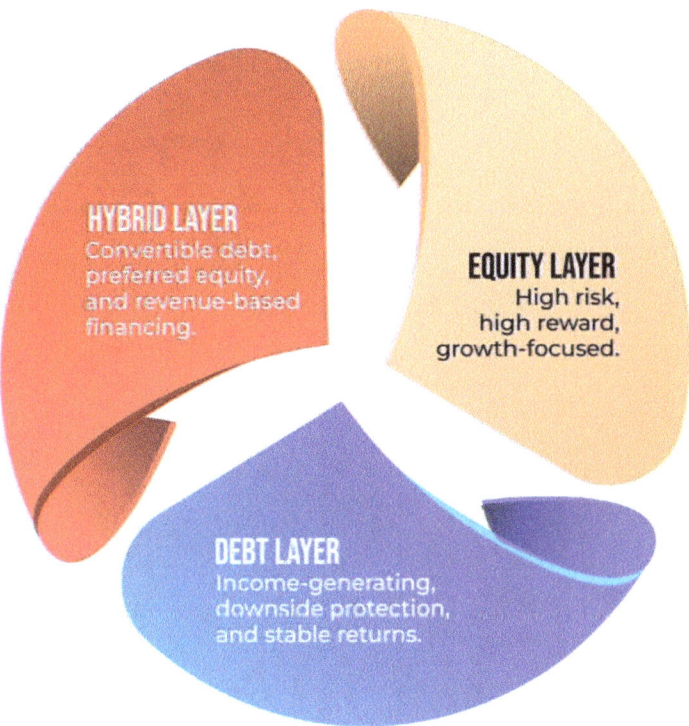

A visual representation of the integrated underwriting approach used in a Full-Stack Venture Capital Funds™

That's real optionality. And it leads to real value not just in exit multiples, but in capital efficiency, team retention, market share, and resilience.

B R O K E N

It also leads to better alignment with Investors. When you can show not just what a company might be worth one day, but what it's generating today, you build trust. And trust, unlike IRR, compounds forever.

The Composite Portfolio Mindset

The traditional venture portfolio is built like a poker table, lots of small bets, a few medium ones, and a couple of big swings. The strategy is diversification through volume.

But a Full-Stack Venture Capital Funds™ is more like a chessboard. Each piece serves a purpose. Some are fast. Some are defensive. Some take time to position. Together, they create a system that's more resilient than any single move.

You might have:

- Early-stage venture bets for high growth.

- Mid-stage companies with structured credit.

- Late-stage businesses using buyout mechanics.

- Asset-light operators with cash flows.

- Real estate or equipment-backed loans for ballast.

This isn't chaos. It's composition. And like a good portfolio manager knows, correlation matters more than concentration.

A New Kind of Venture Discipline

Full-Stack Venture Capital Funds™ investing doesn't mean giving up on innovation. It means applying discipline to innovation. It's not about lowering ambition. It's about raising standards.

You still look for great founders. You still back big ideas. But you do it with a toolkit that protects capital while unlocking it. You do it with a structure that values both cash flow and compounding. And you do it knowing that your job is to deliver returns, not ride trends.

In this world, Venture Capital stops being a storytelling contest and becomes a capital-efficiency exercise. You're not trying to beat the odds. You're engineering the odds to be in your favor.

And that, in the end, is what separates the next generation of funds from the last.

The structural shift toward Full-Stack Venture Capital Funds™ isn't just a clever rebrand. It's a necessary evolution. We can no longer rely on the Venture Capital playbook written for a world of zero interest rates, infinite runway, and endless exit froth.

By embracing income and appreciation together, avoiding vintage risk, optimizing payback periods, and escaping binary outcomes, we unlock a model that is built to last.

Not just for Investors. Not just for founders. But for the future of innovation itself.

Chapter 4

The Capital Efficiency Flywheel

Part 1: Real Yield Through Structured Credit and Dividend Models

Ask any limited partner in a traditional venture fund what they dread most, and somewhere between "capital calls at the wrong time" and "no visibility into exits," you'll find this little monster lurking in the shadows: yield starvation. For decades, Venture Capital has asked Investors to play a long game with short updates. You wire money. You wait. You hear about markups. You wait some more. Then, maybe, there's an exit. Maybe not.

That "maybe" is getting harder to stomach.

Full-Stack Venture Capital Funds™, when designed thoughtfully, does something that feels like heresy in the venture world: it pays investors while the portfolio is still building. In other words, real yield. Monthly or quarterly. Cash-on-cash. No fantasy valuations required.

The typical structured credit model looks something like this. The fund provides a revenue-based loan or an interest-only note to a growth-stage company. In exchange, the company pays a fixed coupon or a percent of revenue, usually with a cap or term limit. If done well, these instruments are senior in the capital stack, secured by receivables, IP, or other business assets, and carry strong covenant protection. For investors, this means predictability. For portfolio companies, it means access to capital without the bloodletting of equity dilution.

Let's say you lend $1 million at 13 percent interest-only for two years. The company pays $130,000 annually in interest. That cash can be used to pay distributions to Investors, cover fund expenses, or be recycled into new deals. And if you add an equity kicker such as warrants, options, or conversion rights, you don't miss out on upside either. This is what we call total return engineering: getting paid while you wait, but not giving up your shot at asymmetric gains.

This model becomes even more powerful in rising interest rate environments where traditional venture multiples compress and exits slow down. Credit becomes not just safer, but also more competitive. Entrepreneurs will pay for speed, certainty, and flexibility. Structured credit delivers all three.

Some critics argue that startups shouldn't be burdened with debt. That's true for early-stage companies with no cash flow. But structured credit isn't meant for pre-seed rounds. It's for companies with predictable revenue, clear customer retention, and repeatable sales. If the company's metrics are strong, a structured loan can actually increase their optionality by letting them grow into their valuation before raising another round.

Dividend models add another layer. If a portfolio company throws off enough cash to pay regular dividends to the fund, you create a self-funding mechanism. Think of it as a perpetual motion machine where investor capital spins off yield, gets redeployed, and compounds. The feedback loop of capital deployment, return, and reinvestment can lead to powerful compounding results over the life of the fund.

Even better, dividend-producing assets help mitigate the "black hole" effect seen in traditional venture structures, where capital goes in but no cash comes out until an unpredictable exit years down the line. This can improve internal rate of return metrics while also providing Investors with much-needed liquidity and confidence.

Dividend strategies also force operational discipline on portfolio companies. When founders know they need to distribute cash regularly, they tend to pay closer attention to gross margins, customer retention, and burn rate. This isn't financial engineering for its own sake; it's a behavioral nudge toward sustainability.

A well-structured dividend and credit strategy doesn't limit innovation. It encourages efficiency, protects downside, and still leaves room for upside. And for investors, it's a relief from the binary outcomes that have defined venture portfolios for too long.

In short, structured credit and dividend models give investors something they haven't had in years: income. And income, unlike markups, is real. It shows up in the bank account, not just the pitch deck.

Part 2: Private Equity-Style Downside Protection

If Venture Capital has been historically defined by its sky-high upside, then private equity has long been the master of not losing money on the way up. It's not that PE doesn't aim for gains; it's that it builds in downside insurance by design. And that's where traditional VC has fallen flat on its face.

Venture funds, especially in the go-go years of the 2010s, started treating equity checks like party favors. Here's some Series A. Need a top-up? Let's bridge you to your next round. No board control. No rights. No real teeth in the documents. The unspoken strategy? Spray money and hope one of the rockets takes off. Everyone else? Written off.

Private equity never bought that logic. Instead, it insisted on terms, controls, and covenants that protected the firm's position even if the growth story didn't go as planned. When you apply those same principles even selectively to innovation-stage capital, you create a powerful new hybrid: an upside-oriented fund that doesn't have to swing for the fences on every single pitch.

Downside protection starts with how you structure the deal. Preferred equity with liquidation preferences is a staple in VC, but few funds press for cumulative dividends, pay-to-play provisions, or board supermajority rights unless they're leading the round. And even then, it's often lip service. A Full-

Stack Venture Capital Funds™ with a private equity lens looks at those terms not as legalese but as levers. Used properly, they give investors a seat at the table when things wobble, and trust me, they always wobble.

Let's take an example. Imagine a fund invests $3 million in a company through a combination of convertible debt and preferred equity. The debt pays 10 percent annually, and the equity includes a 1x participating liquidation preference with seniority over common. If the company goes sideways or sells for a modest exit, that structure allows the fund to recover its initial investment and yield before others see a dime. But if the company does take off, the equity converts and participates in the upside. That's not gambling. That's intelligent structuring.

Private equity also insists on governance. Not because they love meetings, but because decision-making matters. A board seat isn't a trophy; it's a tripwire. It ensures investors have visibility into the business, a say in major decisions, and the power to intervene before problems metastasize. In the venture world, too many board seats are held by people who bring name recognition instead of operational rigor. A Full-Stack Venture Capital Funds™ mindset flips that script. It focuses on performance, accountability, and value creation, not just valuation inflation.

Then there's the use of collateral. Venture-backed companies rarely pledge assets. Most of them don't even think of their intellectual property as leverageable. But with a structured credit overlay, you can create lending arrangements that secure your capital with IP, receivables, or even customer contracts. In a default scenario, that security gives you options. In a wind-down, it gives you negotiating power. And in all cases, it puts you closer to the top of the stack.

This kind of protection changes behavior not just for fund managers, but for founders. When capital comes with accountability, founders tend to use it more wisely. They think about burn multiples, unit economics, and sustainable growth, not just blitzscaling. Ironically, adding structure doesn't stifle innovation; it channels it more effectively.

Private equity downside structures also encourage real diligence. Not the kind where someone spends 72 hours with a data room and a glass of scotch. The real kind. Asking about contingent liabilities. Reviewing customer churn rates. Understanding working capital cycles. This level of scrutiny has been missing in a VC world obsessed with speed and FOMO. And that's one reason why so many funds now hold portfolios filled with overhyped, underperforming companies they barely understood when they wired the money.

Full-Stack Venture Capital Funds™ borrows this diligence discipline from PE and marries it to the venture playbook. The result? A smarter portfolio. Not necessarily one with fewer risks but one with better risk-adjusted returns. Because downside protection isn't about avoiding risk altogether, it's about knowing which risks to take and which to neutralize.

And let's not forget the psychological benefit. Investors sleep better when they know terms, covenants, or collateral protect their capital. In an age when mark-to-market valuations can vanish overnight, having built-in protections feels like holding a parachute instead of a lottery ticket.

Downside protection also accelerates fund-level returns. If you can get your money back from one investment through debt service or liquidation preferences, you free up dry powder to deploy elsewhere. This starts the capital efficiency flywheel all over again. Protect the base. Capture the upside. Repeat.

Ultimately, this blend of venture vision and private equity discipline is what the modern capital stack needs. Not just courage to chase big ideas, but the wisdom to protect the capital that chases them.

Part 3: Income: Generating Assets as a Companion to Venture

Suppose traditional Venture Capital is a high-wire act with no safety net. In that case, income-generating assets are the financial equivalent of wearing a parachute and building an airbag into your landing pad. They don't just smooth out the ride, they redefine what the ride is supposed to be.

Let's start with the obvious: Venture Capital is inherently illiquid. Investors lock up their capital for 10–12 years and cross their fingers for a meaningful liquidity event somewhere down the line. The trouble is, "somewhere down the line" now increasingly looks like never. Exits are delayed. IPO windows are shut. M&A markets are cautious. As a result, Investors sit in limbo, funds strain under the J-curve, and fund managers are stuck explaining why their portfolios look like a bunch of pretty logos but no cash flows.

Enter income-generating assets. These are not designed to replace Venture Capital, they're designed to support it. Think of them as ballast in a sailboat. While the venture engine is aiming for the wind, the income layer keeps the vessel stable and upright.

The most common income strategies layered into Full-Stack Venture Capital Funds™ include structured credit (which we covered in Part 1), revenue-based financing, asset-backed lending, royalty streams, and high-margin service businesses tucked into the platform. None of these are flashy. None of them gets you on the cover of TechCrunch. But they do something far more valuable: they put money back in the fund's pocket while the rest of the portfolio matures.

Let's say your fund invests in a digital health platform but also underwrites a companion services business that provides white-labeled telehealth operations to clinics. The Venture Capital side aims for massive upside if the platform scales. But the services business? It pays a dividend. It generates cash flow. It covers part of the management fee or even contributes to investor distributions.

You don't need everything in the portfolio to be a unicorn. You just need enough cash flow somewhere to fund the journey of the unicorns.

This hybrid mindset reflects a deeper truth that many Venture Capitalists still deny: cash flow and innovation are not mutually exclusive. In fact, many of the best businesses on earth, think Adobe, Salesforce, and Shopify, generated meaningful income before they ever IPO'd. The obsession with "growth at all costs" has distorted the lens. In reality, sustainable growth and monetization discipline often go hand in hand. Income-generating assets build that muscle inside the fund.

They also allow fund managers to be more strategic. Instead of being forced to exit a great company prematurely just to show DPI (Distributions to Paid-In Capital) to Investors, a manager with income from other parts of the portfolio can afford to wait. That patience often results in higher multiples and better outcomes, not just for the investment but for the entire fund.

And there's a second-order effect worth noting: income-generating assets reduce reliance on future fundraisers. When cash is coming in regularly, managers aren't constantly begging Investors for their next vintage. This creates a virtuous cycle of autonomy, flexibility, and long-term thinking. You don't need to inflate valuations to show paper gains. You don't need to push portfolio companies into fundraising cycles just to mark up your position. The fund becomes a true steward of capital, not a cheerleader for the next round.

Let's bring this down to a micro level. Imagine your fund makes 20 investments. Five are high-growth tech startups. Five are royalty-backed consumer brands. Five are revenue-financed SaaS companies. And five are opportunistic service providers that generate free cash flow and modest growth. Venture-style companies might take 7 to 10 years to mature. But the others? They're paying off in quarters, not decades.

This creates flexibility in portfolio construction. You can recycle capital from income-generating positions into higher-risk bets without doing capital calls. You can meet your preferred return hurdles faster. You can even defend your valuation marks with real earnings, which makes audit season far less harrowing.

There's also a signaling benefit. Income pays. Literally, but it also shows discipline. It tells investors you're building a business, not just a bet. And when those investors are family offices, RIAs, or other private wealth channels that value steady returns, the ability to point to yield, not just narrative, becomes a massive differentiator.

Critics may argue that income-generating businesses are "boring." And maybe they are. But I'll take boring cash in the bank over exciting paper gains any day of the week. Boring keeps the lights on. Boring gives you dry powder. Boring funds the bets that change the world.

It also attracts a different caliber of co-investors. Smart capital often chases stability over volatility. When a fund shows consistent internal distributions, it becomes an easier yes for wealth managers, family offices, and even institutional Investors with conservative mandates. That's not a bug, it's a feature.

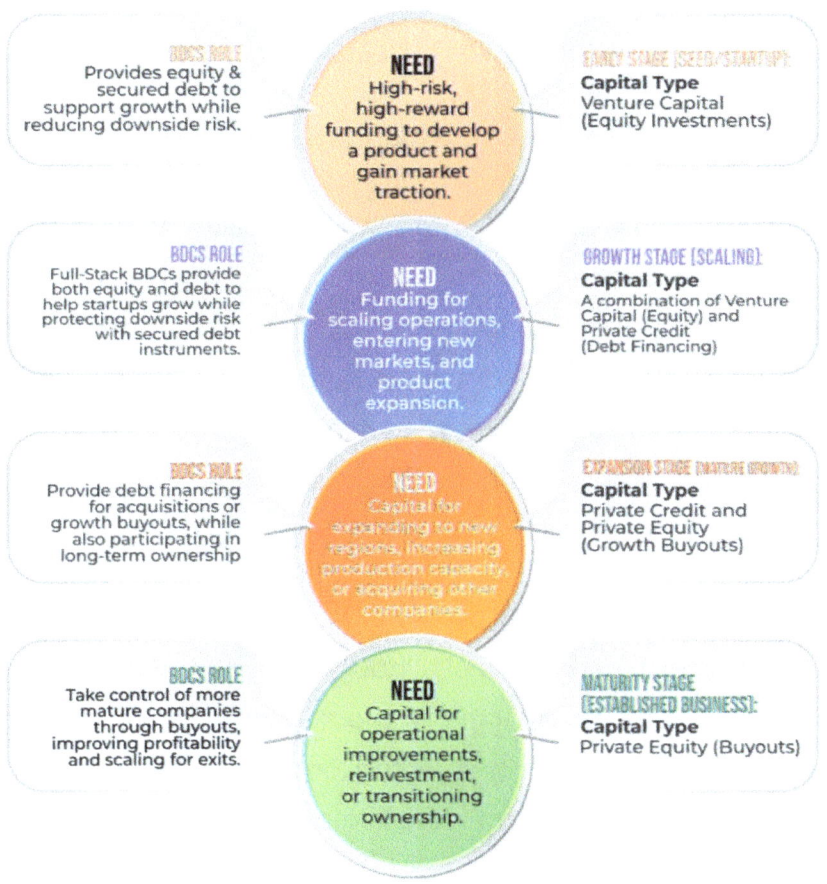

How Full-Stack VC Funds support companies across each stage of growth, combining equity, structured credit, and buyouts to provide the right capital at the right time.

In the end, income-generating assets make a venture portfolio more resilient, more dynamic, and frankly, more honest. They expose what's working now, not what might work someday. And they give fund managers breathing room to nurture the next big thing without betting the entire house on a single hand.

Venture doesn't need to be binary. It can be beautifully blended. Income-generating assets are how you get there.

Part 4: Redefining Alpha in a Blended Strategy Environment

For decades, "alpha" in Venture Capital was a one-dimensional chase. Find the next unicorn. Back it early. Pray it goes public. Hope your logo ends up in the pitch deck of the next fund. That was the formula. Returns were measured in multiples of invested capital, but more often than not, they were also measured in hype, headlines, and how close you could get to Sand Hill Road royalty.

But in the world we live in now, that definition of alpha no longer works. Markets are cyclical. IPO windows shut. Growth slows. Markups mean little if there's no path to liquidity. Investors are no longer dazzled by logos; they're demanding distributions. They want real value, not just perceived momentum. That means alpha must evolve. And in a blended strategy, Full-Stack Venture Capital Funds™ already has.

Alpha today is about generating superior risk-adjusted returns across a mix of assets. It's not just about picking winners. It's about building a portfolio that can perform in up markets, down markets, and stagnant markets. That requires rethinking everything from deal sourcing to capital structure to liquidity pathways.

Let's start with portfolio construction. In a pure-play venture fund, the barbell strategy rules; lots of moonshots, lots of write-offs, and maybe one or two monsters that carry the fund. But in a Full-Stack Venture Capital Funds™, alpha doesn't rely on outliers. It compounds across the entire capital stack.

You might generate consistent returns through structured credit, opportunistic exits via secondaries, and long-term upside through preferred equity with smart conversion rights. Add in a handful of dividend-yielding assets and an occasional private equity-style buyout or roll-up, and suddenly your fund has multiple engines running. Alpha, in this context, is not found at the end of a rainbow. It's built block by block, quarter by quarter, from both growth and income.

This model also changes your relationship to time. In a traditional venture structure, most returns are backloaded. That's fine when capital is cheap and Investors are patient. But in a high-rate, liquidity-sensitive environment, time is a cost. Every quarter you don't return capital is a quarter your internal rate of return decays. A Full-Stack Venture Capital Funds™ combats this decay by pushing forward distributions. Yield generation starts early. Recycling kicks in sooner. Dry powder gets replenished continuously.

This continuous motion is where the flywheel effect begins to show up. Distributions reinvested become new bets. New bets funded internally reduce dilution. Less dilution increases returns. Returns fuel distributions. And so on. Alpha becomes a function of momentum, not just magic.

Let's also talk about the downside. Traditional venture managers tend to ignore it. They're trained to swing for the fences. But Full-Stack Venture Capital Funds™ managers know that limiting losses is just as important as chasing gains. That's why every investment is structured with care. That's why covenants exist. That's why you underwrite not just the founder's vision, but the business model's resilience.

Alpha, in this blended world, is the ability to see around corners to know which companies need debt, which need equity, and which need both. It's knowing when to convert, when to hold, and when to exit. It's the judgment to recognize a 3x return today is better than chasing a mythical 10x tomorrow. That kind of discretion doesn't get headlines, but it does get results.

There's also an element of alpha that comes from fund-level innovation. How you manage cash. How you report performance. How you negotiate fees with service providers. These are not deal-specific actions, but they contribute directly to outcomes. A well-run fund extracts alpha from every lever available, not just the deal sheet.

Then there's sourcing. In a blended fund, you're not constrained to the same pipeline as every other venture firm. You can look at companies that are too mature for seed-stage funds but not ready for private equity. You can find off-market lending opportunities with embedded equity options. You can back founders with profitable businesses who've been overlooked because they didn't fit the "hypergrowth" narrative. That's where some of the best alpha lives in the blind spots of traditional funds.

Finally, let's redefine the alpha experience for Investors. It's not just about IRR or TVPI. It's about confidence. It's about predictability. It's about the ability to see cash come back while still holding upside. When you give investors a portfolio that delivers both yield and growth, both liquidity and long-term appreciation, you give them peace of mind. And peace of mind in capital markets is one of the rarest and most valuable assets of all.

Alpha is not a number on a spreadsheet. It's a philosophy. It's how you approach risk, time, capital, and opportunity. In the old model, it was about who you knew and how early you got in. In the new model, it's about how well you allocate, how smartly you structure, and how reliably you deliver.

That's the alpha that lasts.

Part 5: The Liquidity Layer: How Interim Returns Sustain Long-Term Vision

Traditional Venture Capital is allergic to liquidity. The entire model is built around patient capital invest early, support relentlessly, wait indefinitely. But while the vision may be long-term, the reality is this: Investors have short-term needs. They manage portfolios with liquidity targets, rebalancing schedules, and distribution expectations. A capital strategy that ignores this tension is not just outdated; it's misaligned.

Enter the liquidity layer.

In a Full-Stack Venture Capital Funds™, the liquidity layer is the part of the portfolio deliberately designed to produce interim returns. This doesn't mean quick flips or shallow bets. It means allocating a portion of capital to instruments and assets with built-in pathways to cash flow, repayment, or monetization, without waiting for an acquisition or IPO.

The most obvious components of the liquidity layer are interest-bearing notes, revenue-based financing, and structured credit. These instruments pay out regularly, often monthly or quarterly, creating a predictable stream of cash into the fund. But the real power of the liquidity layer comes when those returns aren't just pocketed, they're recycled.

Recycling is the secret weapon here. Every dollar that returns early can be redeployed. That means your capital doesn't just sit idle between investments or exits. It gets a second, and sometimes a third, life. Over time, this dramatically enhances capital efficiency. The same $1 million can support multiple investments over the life of the fund, compounding your exposure to upside while offsetting risk with steady repayments.

Let's take an example. Suppose your fund makes a $500,000 structured credit investment in a growth-stage business. Over two years, that note pays back $150,000 in interest and $500,000 in principal. You take that repaid capital and deploy it into another investment with a similar structure. Do it again. By the end of the fund's life, that original $500,000 might have backed three different companies, generated $450,000 in interest, and still retained equity kickers in each. You've effectively multiplied your deployment leverage without increasing your capital base.

This is what makes the liquidity layer a flywheel enabler. As interest and repayments come back, you feed them into new opportunities. That momentum creates more chances for returns and more protection against dry spells in venture exits.

But there's another benefit. Interim liquidity smooths volatility at the fund level. In traditional venture capital, fund returns often look like a flat line followed by a sudden spike (or not). That creates IRR drag, investor anxiety, and fundraising challenges. When you have a liquidity layer, your return profile becomes a staircase instead of a cliff. Distributions appear earlier, are smoother, and occur more often. Investors gain confidence. Fund managers gain flexibility.

Liquidity also gives you leverage in negotiations. If you know your fund has incoming cash flow, you can be more patient with certain deals and more aggressive in others. You can bridge a company temporarily without tapping your Investors. You can say no to a down round. You can fund an opportunistic acquisition quickly because you're not waiting on a capital call. In short, liquidity gives you posture. And posture gives you power.

Some critics will argue that introducing liquidity compromises long-term vision. That it makes funds too focused on yield or short-term wins. But in reality, it does the opposite. It creates breathing room. It allows fund managers to wait longer on moonshots because they're not under pressure to generate all returns from one direction. It creates optionality without sacrificing ambition.

Think of it like ballast in a ship. Without it, you're at the mercy of the waves. With it, you're stable, steady, and free to chart bold courses.

This is especially important in today's market environment. Liquidity events are fewer and farther between. Exit timelines have been extended. Investors are more selective. In this world, having a liquidity layer is not a luxury; it's a necessity.

And it's not just about credit instruments. The liquidity layer can include preferred equity with redemption rights, secondary sales, dividend streams from mature portfolio companies, and even strategic licensing deals that produce royalty payments. Anything that generates cash flow without requiring a full-blown exit adds to the layer.

The real innovation, however, is how this layer integrates with the rest of the fund. It's not siloed. It's not just a "safe" sleeve while the rest of the fund swings for the fences. It's part of a holistic system, one that balances near-term cash needs with long-term growth bets. One that honors the ambitions of founders without ignoring the responsibilities to investors.

In a world where venture funds are increasingly under pressure to prove relevance, the liquidity layer offers an edge. It's a way to deliver trust. To demonstrate mastery. To show that capital allocation isn't just a gamble, it's a craft.

Because the truth is, liquidity isn't the enemy of vision. It's what makes vision sustainable.

Part 6: Behavioral Efficiency: How Capital Design Shapes Founders' Choices

Talk to enough venture-backed founders and you'll start to see a troubling pattern. Many of them, even the brilliant ones, optimize for the wrong things. Topline growth at all costs. Splashy valuations over sustainable economics. Press headlines instead of profit margins. But these choices aren't necessarily irrational. They're a product of the system they've been fed, a system that rewards signaling over substance.

The kind of capital you raise influences the kind of company you build.

Traditional Venture Capital, for all its power, often encourages behavior that is growth-obsessed but financially reckless. It's a binary game: build a rocket ship or die trying. That creates distorted incentives. Founders are told to "raise more, faster" even when their unit economics are shaky. They're pushed to scale teams, burn cash, and chase vanity metrics to justify their next round, not because it's the best strategy, but because it's the expected one.

This is where capital structure becomes more than a financial decision. It becomes a behavioral one.

When you bring in structured credit, revenue-based finance, preferred equity with distributions, or dividend models, you send a very different signal to founders. You're not just handing them money, you're handing them expectations. Expectations around efficiency, discipline, and sustainability. And those expectations change how companies behave.

Let's take a simple example: a founder raises $2 million in equity with no cash obligations. What do they do? They spend it. Fast. Growth is the imperative, burn is a badge of honor, and they'll worry about profitability later, maybe. Now imagine that same founder raises $1 million in equity and $1 million in structured credit with monthly interest payments. What happens now? They think harder. They project cash flow more carefully. They hire slower. They prioritize paying customers over press coverage. They might still chase growth, but they do it with a sharper pencil.

This isn't just conjecture. Studies in behavioral economics show that constraints can create focus. When founders know capital must be repaid, they make different choices. They delay vanity hires. They hold marketing accountable. They run leaner, meaner operations not because they're afraid, but because the structure encourages it.

This is behavioral efficiency in action. The idea that financial design influences operational behavior.

And here's the kicker: companies built under these constraints often end up stronger. They survive downturns. They pivot more effectively. They don't rely on endless rounds of equity just to stay alive. And when they do exit, they do so with cleaner cap tables, better margins, and happier investors.

Behavioral efficiency also improves communication between founders and funders. When expectations are grounded in real cash flows instead of speculative valuations, conversations become more honest. Investors don't just ask for KPIs they ask for collections rates, churn mitigation, and burn multiples. Founders learn to manage their companies like businesses, not just products. The relationship shifts from cheerleading to coaching.

This is not about micromanagement. It's about clarity. When a founder knows their funding partner expects accountability, they rise to the challenge. Not all of them, of course, but the ones who do tend to build more durable companies.

Capital structure even shapes culture. A startup fueled by high-octane equity alone often develops a "spend to survive" culture. But a startup funded through blended capital, some of which requires repayment or distribution, builds a "build to last" mindset. That trickles down to every department. Marketing spends more carefully. Product focuses on monetizable features. Finance becomes a core function earlier.

The best part? These companies are often just as innovative. They don't sacrifice vision; they sharpen it. By removing the pressure to constantly impress investors with vanity metrics, founders can return to building for real customers. Real markets. Real needs.

Of course, behavioral efficiency doesn't eliminate risk. Startups will still fail. Markets will still shift. But when the capital stack nudges founders toward better decisions, the odds improve. The losses shrink. The upside gets cleaner. The portfolio becomes less of a lottery and more of a strategic mosaic.

And from an investor's standpoint, behavioral efficiency increases signal fidelity. You start to see who the real builders are, not just the best fundraisers. You start to identify which teams are resilient, not just lucky. This improves portfolio curation over time, especially in multi-fund strategies.

There's also a psychological dividend. Founders who operate with financial discipline tend to burn out less. They experience less pressure. They don't live or die by the next round. They become long-term leaders in a marathon rather than short-term sprinters.

In the end, this is the quiet power of capital design. It's not just about where money comes from. It's about what that money teaches. Smart capital doesn't just fund the business, it shapes it.

When your portfolio companies are learning the right lessons, you're not just managing capital. You're building a better ecosystem.

Part 7: Redefining Alpha in a Blended Strategy Environment

Venture Capital once held a monopoly on a particular kind of mystique, the notion that "alpha" meant backing the next Uber, Stripe, or OpenAI. The formula was intoxicating; swing hard, miss often, but land one monster win, and all sins are forgiven. That model worked when the cost of capital was low, the tech sector was on a tear, and Investors were comfortable with long lockups and binary outcomes. But that era is fading fast.

Today, "alpha" needs a new definition, one built not on unicorn hunting but on intelligent capital engineering. It's no longer enough to ask how high your winners fly. The better question is: how often do you get your money back with a return, and how much of that return comes in the form of actual cash flow, not just marked-up valuations?

In a blended strategy environment where venture equity is paired with structured credit, yield-oriented instruments, and private equity tools, alpha is no longer a one-dimensional metric. It becomes multidimensional: a fusion of consistent income, risk-adjusted appreciation, strategic control, and optionality at exit.

Let's unpack this.

Traditional alpha measures often focus on MOIC (Multiple on Invested Capital) and IRR (Internal Rate of Return). But these metrics can be gamed. A company that raises at a higher valuation in a frothy market looks great on paper until that markup evaporates or the exit never comes. Mark-to-market isn't real until it's monetized. Worse, many funds don't distribute proceeds quickly, meaning Investors can't reinvest or reallocate efficiently.

Blended strategies change the game.

First, Full-Stack Venture Capital Funds™ models deliver consistent, realized alpha to investors through dividends, interest payments, and partial exits. That means you're not just accruing value; you're capturing it. When a structured loan pays 13% annually, that return is real and repeatable. It doesn't depend on an acquisition or IPO. It shows up in distributions, not just dashboards.

Second, blended strategies optimize for risk-adjusted alpha. A 5x return on a highly volatile startup with no governance rights and no board seat might sound great until the whole thing implodes in year three. Compare that to a 2x return on a structured equity deal with downside protection, collateral rights, and consistent income. Which one is the smarter investment? In a volatile world, preservation of capital is the foundation of real alpha.

Third, there's a strategic alpha value derived from deal structure, governance influence, and operational leverage. The ability to renegotiate terms, trigger protective provisions, or step in during periods of distress can create value far beyond what's seen in headline multiples. Most venture funds don't have this kind of leverage. Full-Stack Venture Capital Funds™ strategies do.

Fourth, consider temporal alpha, the velocity of capital recycling. If you can turn capital faster through partial repayments, dividends, or asset sales, your capital efficiency increases. You don't have to wait seven to ten years for a mythical exit. You can compound earlier, deploy more nimbly, and respond to market cycles with greater agility. This flexibility is itself a source of outperformance.

And finally, there's behavioral alpha the compounded impact of funding companies in ways that promote discipline, sustainability, and smarter decision-making. As we explored in Part 6, behavioral design in capital structures influences founder actions. Companies that operate with financial rigor tend to outperform over time, especially in turbulent markets. That's alpha created not by luck or hype, but by design.

The traditional view of alpha big bets, binary outcomes, and hope as a strategy isn't just outdated. It's dangerous in the current macro environment. Investors are demanding more than just paper gains. They want strategies that produce income, preserve capital, and create a realistic path to liquidity. A Full-Stack Venture Capital Funds™ is answering that call by creating multi-source alpha: appreciation from equity, yield from credit, and durability from structure.

This approach also recalibrates how fund managers evaluate their own performance. It's no longer about chasing unicorns. It's about building a portfolio that behaves like a well-balanced machine: some parts generating yield, others compounding equity growth, all contributing to fund-level resilience. In this world, a 3x net return to investors with consistent quarterly distributions and low volatility might be more impressive and more repeatable than a single 50x outlier.

Even portfolio construction changes. With multiple tools in their toolbox, fund managers can segment investments by risk, return profile, and time horizon. That allows for strategic balancing using credit to generate income, equity to capture upside, and private equity tools to protect capital. The result is a more stable return stream and a more resilient fund.

And from the founder's perspective, this redefinition of alpha is liberating. They no longer have to contort their business around unrealistic growth trajectories just to fit the VC mold. Instead, they can focus on building real companies with real economics and still attract high-quality capital. When capital becomes a partner in value creation rather than a rocket fuel dispenser, outcomes improve across the board.

In a blended strategy environment offered by Full-Stack Venture Capital Funds™, alpha is no longer about finding the next Facebook. It's about engineering outcomes through smarter structures, better behavior, and capital-efficient models. It's about creating value you can measure, capture, and repeat, not just dream about.

Part 8: The Flywheel in Motion

The magic of a Full-Stack Venture Capital Funds™ strategy isn't just in the components, it's in the motion. Structured credit, preferred equity, income-generating assets, and growth-stage venture deals are each powerful on their own. But when synchronized within an evergreen, total return model, they become a capital-efficiency flywheel, a system that compounds intelligently, distributes predictably, and outperforms across cycles.

Let's walk through how this works over time.

Year 1: Capital is deployed across yield-oriented investments: structured credit with seniority and protections, dividend-generating operating companies, and a measured entry into equity positions that carry long-term upside. But unlike traditional VC, investors don't wait in the dark. Income begins immediately, with interest, revenue shares, or dividends flowing back into the fund quarterly. These proceeds aren't decorative; they're fuel. They pay distributions, cover fund expenses, and get recycled into new deals. The fund is already moving.

Year 2: The income engine is humming. Early investments are seasoning, with some equity-linked instruments converting or triggering optional milestones. As the fund raises more capital, it's using internal cash flow to expand. This reduces dependency on the next vintage and avoids pressure to chase frothy deals just to deploy. Investors begin to feel the rhythm: cash back while still capturing upside. Meanwhile, the fund's internal capital base grows, creating more velocity and control.

Years 3 to 5: The flywheel gains speed. More portfolio companies are generating steady distributions. Some early equity positions are beginning to appreciate, but the fund isn't under pressure to sell. It's evergreen, patient, and selective. Strategic partial exits may occur, especially where gains can be locked in to feed the cycle. At the same time, new deals continue to be backed not just by new dry powder, but also by recycled returns. The capital base thickens, not thins. Investors see real, cash-on-cash returns while their NAV steadily climbs. This dual engine income plus appreciation becomes the new normal.

Years 6 to 10: The fund's structure shows its full strength. No sunset date forces artificial exits. Venture Capital positions that needed time to mature are now peaking. When exits come, they're strategic, not rushed. The big multiples show up, and the patient capital behind them gets rewarded. Meanwhile, the yield-producing assets haven't stopped working. In fact, they've expanded, with cash flow from previous cycles seeding new ones. Distributions continue, while NAV appreciates. The flywheel no longer needs pushing it turns on its own.

Beyond Year 10: This isn't the end. It's the evolution. The fund is self-funding, evergreen, and continuously compounding. The next generation of companies is already under management, financed from returns rather than just new investor commitments. For long-term investors, this is the holy grail: a vehicle that delivers both liquidity and longevity. No need to commit to new fund vintages or wait for final distributions from a sunset fund. The same capital remains at work growing, yielding, compounding.

This is a total return system, not a hope-for-the-best vehicle. It redefines what capital efficiency looks like in the innovation economy. It provides Investors with visibility, control, and yield without giving up exposure to transformational Venture Capital upside. It creates time alignment with founders, fund managers, and investors. It rewards patience, precision, and discipline.

In a world where too many funds chase headlines, this approach builds outcomes. While others race to raise the next fund, the flywheel keeps moving forward quietly, efficiently, relentlessly. It doesn't need to shout. The returns speak for themselves.

Rewiring the Venture Model for Smarter, Stronger Returns

The traditional Venture Capital model of high burn, long waits, and binary outcomes wasn't built for today's investor or today's economy. It was built for a time when growth was cheap, exits were frequent, and capital was patient because it had no other options. That time is over.

What today's investors want and deserve is not just potential. They want performance. They want cash flow without sacrificing upside. They want durability without dulling innovation. They want a structure that reflects the full range of opportunities across the capital stack, not just spray-and-pray equity bets.

This chapter introduced the Full-Stack Venture Capital Funds™: a model that combines structured credit, downside-protected equity, income-generating operating assets, and long-hold venture opportunities into a single, disciplined system. It's a flywheel because it feeds itself. It builds momentum, recycles capital, and compounds returns. It doesn't rely on blind faith or 10-year luck. It relies on architecture.

By emphasizing income early, enforcing discipline through structure, and removing artificial timelines through evergreen design, this approach reframes what "Venture

Capital" can mean. It becomes not just a home-run game but a "Money Ball" type of total-return game winning lineup. Not just risk-on, but risk-managed. Not just occasional liquidity, but regular cash-on-cash returns with terminal-value optionality.

This is the future for those bold enough to leave the old model behind. For investors willing to trade narrative for numbers. For founders who prefer durability to drama. And for fund managers who believe that performance is built, not bet.

The Full-Stack Venture Capital Funds™ isn't theoretical, it's operational. And for those who've seen it in motion, there's no going back.

Chapter 5

Better for Founders – A More Aligned Capital Model

Part 1: The Death of the "Next Round" Mindset

For too long, the startup ecosystem has revolved around a single, unspoken rule: survive until your next raise. Everything, hiring, marketing, and even product design was subordinated to this cyclical pressure. Founders became pitch artists first, CEOs second. The health of the company was measured not by profitability or customer retention, but by valuation markup and who led the last round.

This "next round or die" dynamic has failed both founders and investors. It creates artificial sprints in businesses that should be run as marathons. It pushes companies into premature scaling, forces them to burn unsustainably, and often results in founders losing control of their vision, their equity, or both.

Enter the Full-Stack Venture Capital Model, with a capital framework built to fund not just a single round but the entire entrepreneurial journey.

This model is a structural shift. It replaces the episodic, binary nature of traditional venture financing with a layered, modular approach. Instead of a founder having to re-pitch the business every 12 to 18 months to survive, a full-stack fund can deploy the right type of capital at the right time: senior credit to finance working capital, revenue-based lending to support growth, preferred equity with protective terms at strategic inflection points, and long-duration equity to fuel enduring innovation.

In a full-stack model, capital is not an event. It's an ongoing relationship.

This unlocks something powerful: founder autonomy. When capital is flexible and continuous, founders don't have to contort their strategy to fit a round. They can build toward real outcomes, profitability, acquisition, or long-term market leadership without having to pause the business to appease a different set of gatekeepers at every stage.

The model also allows for a smarter matching of capital to use. You don't fund inventory with equity. You don't finance user acquisition with dilution. You don't force a founder to sell a piece of their company to do something that a loan or a royalty agreement could cover. The full-stack approach brings precision to funding decisions, backed by a full menu of instruments rather than just a Series A term sheet.

And for the founder, this precision leads to preservation: of equity, of control, of mission.

Beyond that, the full-stack model encourages the kind of businesses we should want more of: profitable, durable, customer-loved companies that create real enterprise value. Founders are no longer coached to ignore profitability in the name of speed. Instead, they're supported with financing that rewards efficiency, not just ambition.

It also lowers emotional volatility. Founders aren't whiplashed by market sentiment. They're not pressured to rise in a down cycle or pretend they're worth a multiple that the market won't support next year. The capital is available when needed and aligned with the company's actual performance.

Importantly, this approach doesn't reject traditional Venture Capital altogether. It recontextualizes it. It treats high-risk, high-reward equity investing as one tool among many, not the only hammer in the toolbox. When equity is used, it's intentional, paired with structure, and part of a broader roadmap.

It turns capital into a strategy, not a scramble.

For founders, this is the difference between being treated like a portfolio bet versus a long-term capital partner. It changes the tone of the relationship. There's less pressure to dazzle and more room to deliver. Founders can plan five years out instead of just trying to survive the next five quarters.

The Full-Stack Venture Capital Funds™ model is not only better capital. It's a better culture. It values founder time, founder energy, and founder equity in ways traditional VC rarely does. It doesn't ask founders to play a game of musical chairs with ever-larger funding rounds. It helps them build a real business and finance it from start to scale to liquidity.

This is how we put an end to the "next round" treadmill. We replace it with a model that actually respects the journey.

Part 2: Using Credit as a Bridge to Profitability or Acquisition

In the legacy Venture Capital playbook, every inflection point, every hiring need, product launch, market expansion, or margin squeeze triggered the same knee-jerk response: raise another equity round. Whether it was the right time or not, you dilute to survive.

But in a Full-Stack Venture Capital model, capital isn't confined to one shape. It comes in multiple forms credit, equity, hybrids and is matched precisely to a company's situation. And one of the most powerful tools in this arsenal is credit.

Credit doesn't just plug gaps. It creates leverage, positioning, and time all of which can dramatically shift the trajectory of a company's growth and its next valuation event.

Imagine a founder whose company has solid recurring revenue, healthy margins, and growing market share but just needs 12 months to reach break-even or unlock the next tier of strategic interest. A traditional equity raise at this stage would be expensive. Valuation would be anchored to current financials. The result? Dilution. Less ownership for founders, early employees, and first-round investors.

Now imagine that the company accesses a $2M structured credit facility on an interest-only basis, with flexible repayment terms and an equity kicker. That capital fuels 12 months of controlled growth, improved metrics, and stronger customer contracts. When it's time to raise equity again, the company isn't negotiating from weakness; it's walking into the market with tailwinds.

The result? A much higher valuation. Less dilution. Better terms. And most importantly, more retained ownership for those who believed early.

This is where credit becomes more than a bridge. It becomes a catalyst for value compression on dilution and expansion of long-term enterprise value.

The next equity round doesn't go away; it just shows up downstream, when the company is larger, stronger, and more valuable. And because the prior funding came with minimal or no dilution, everyone from founders to early backers retains a larger slice of a much larger pie.

Even in acquisition scenarios, this shift in timing matters. Companies that can say "not yet" to a modest exit often end up in dramatically better conversations later. Credit extends their option runway. It lets them be acquired when they're ready, not when their bank account forces them to.

And for investors who hold both the credit and equity exposure, this sequencing creates an elegant return profile: income early, upside later, and downside protection throughout.

The takeaway is this: credit isn't a compromise. It's a strategic enabler. It lets founders *skip* the desperation round, *set up* the premium round, and *control* the story all the way to the endgame.

In a Full-Stack Venture Capital Funds™ model, credit isn't a one-off tactic it's part of a deliberate architecture. One designed to amplify upside, reduce unnecessary dilution, and fund the entire journey from product to profit to premium exit.

Part 3: Non-Dilutive Solutions and Capital Stack Creativity

One of the most dangerous myths in the startup ecosystem is that equity is the only real form of venture funding. Founders are conditioned to believe that dilution is inevitable and that each step forward must come with a sacrifice of ownership. But in a Full-Stack Venture Capital Funds™ model, equity is only one tool in a larger kit, and often the most expensive one.

Instead of defaulting to equity, a capital-efficient venture fund asks: *what is the company solving for right now?* Is it cash flow to fulfill orders? Is it time to reach break-even? Is it capital to expand into a new market with proven unit economics? Not every challenge requires giving up another 20% of the company.

This is where non-dilutive solutions come into play. Revenue-based financing, equipment leasing, accounts receivable lines, milestone-tied credit facilities, and even grant-matching or government-backed loans all offer capital without touching the cap table. And when applied with precision, they allow founders to move faster, prove more, and raise equity on far better terms *if* and *when* they decide to.

CAPITAL STACK STRUCTURE

NON-DILUTIVE CAPITAL

Non-dilutive options like revenue-based financing, working capital lines of credit, and equipment leasing. These options provide growth capital without affecting ownership.

STRUCTURED CREDIT

Includes venture debt, interest-only loans, or revenue-based financing

PREFERRED EQUITY

It is used for strategic growth, to accelerate scaling or acquisitions.

EQUITY INVESTMENTS

Equity investments are reserved for long-term upside potential and are used selectively

A visual breakdown of how Full-Stack Venture Capital Funds™ deploy capital: beginning with non-dilutive tools at the top, followed by structured credit, preferred equity, and equity investments.

A well-architected capital stack blends these options into a tailored financial strategy. For example, a company may use:

- A revenue-based loan to support product fulfillment,

- A line of credit to manage working capital cycles,

- An interest-only venture debt facility to support expansion,

- And preferred equity only when it's time to accelerate scale and dominate a market.

This capital stack doesn't just preserve ownership, it optimizes the *timing* and *cost* of capital. It creates breathing room for founders, a runway for operational milestones, and leverage in downstream negotiations.

It also sends a signal to the market: this company is *well-capitalized*, *capital-efficient*, and *capital-savvy*. Strategic acquirers and institutional investors pay attention to how a company finances its growth. Those who demonstrate smart use of leverage, strong repayment discipline, and milestone-aligned capital raise rounds are far more attractive than those who burned through equity too early and too cheaply.

Importantly, this layered capital approach also aligns the fund's interests with the company's trajectory. A Full-Stack Venture Capital Funds™ benefits from early yield on credit, participation in long-term upside via equity or warrants, and the ability to redeploy returned capital dynamically. The flywheel turns faster. Value creation becomes intentional, not incidental.

And there's a deeper cultural shift here, too. When founders are supported with creative, non-dilutive financing instead of pressure to fundraise at every turn, they tend to stay more focused on customers, products, and profits. They become operators first, and capital seekers second.

In other words, they stop running a fundraising business and start running *the actual business.*

That's what a Full-Stack Venture Capital Funds™ enables. It isn't just about money, it's about *freedom.* The freedom to choose when, how, and whether to raise equity. The freedom to say no to the wrong terms. The freedom to grow on your own timeline.

And in the long run, that freedom creates companies that are not only more resilient but more rewarding to everyone involved.

Part 4: When Founders Become Partners, Not Just Portfolio Companies

In the old VC model, founders are assets. At best, they're talented stewards of the capital you provide. At worst, they're liabilities you need to replace. Either way, the relationship is transactional. You invest; they execute. You track KPIs, they race the clock. And when the clock runs out, they either hit a home run or strike out and get recapitalized, replaced, or shut down.

But this is the wrong mental model especially in a world where capital is no longer scarce, but alignment is.

In a Full-Stack Venture Capital Funds™ model, founders are not just bet-takers. They're partners. And the relationship is built on something deeper than valuation: shared incentives and strategic alignment over time.

That starts with how capital is deployed. When the fund provides structured credit instead of dilutive equity, it sends a powerful message: *we believe in your ability to generate cash flow, not just a future exit.* When dividends or revenue-sharing terms are part of the deal, it says: *we're not just here for the endgame, we want to build value together today.*

This approach changes how founders think about their investors. Instead of seeing VCs as gatekeepers or distant stakeholders waiting for liquidity events, they start to see them as true collaborators, people invested in their success, not just their optionality.

- And when founders feel like partners, their behavior shifts.

- They don't chase hype. They chase margins.

- They don't inflate burn. They optimize return.

- They don't play valuation games. They build enduring businesses that can support debt, reward equity, and scale profitably.

Even better, this partnership mindset fosters longer, healthier relationships. Instead of trying to "graduate" from one investor to the next every 18 months, founders can grow with the same fund over the years, since that fund has the capital to support each phase of the journey. Credit in the early growth years. Equity for scale. Hybrid solutions for acquisitions or roll-ups. Structured exits through redemptions or revenue recapture.

It's a new type of founder journey *co-built, not just financed.*

And when a founder truly believes their investor is in the trenches with them, they pick up the phone more. They ask for help earlier. They listen, adjust, and execute better. Not because they're under pressure but because they're respected, supported, and empowered.

This is especially powerful in venture portfolios where repeat founders and serial operators drive outsize returns. The full-stack model earns long-term trust by showing up with the right capital at the right time, not just a term sheet and a timer.

Let's be clear: alignment doesn't mean softness. You still negotiate. You still enforce terms. You still have governance protections and performance expectations. But those mechanisms exist *within* a shared vision, not in opposition to it.

When done right, the relationship between fund and founder starts to look less like landlord and tenant and more like co-owners of the same building, both with skin in the game, both working to increase the value of the structure, and both reaping the rewards together.

And over time, this kind of capital partnership pays off. Not just in returns, but in reputation. Founders talk. They share who treated them fairly. Who stepped in when it mattered? Who created real value, not just cap table pressure?

The next generation of iconic companies will not be built *on* founders. They will be built in *collaboration with* them.

That's the real promise of the Full-Stack Venture Capital Funds™ Model.

Chapter 6

Better for Investors – Smarter, Safer, Stronger Returns

Part 1: The Changing Psychology of Investors

There was a time when Investors treated Venture Capital like a black box that could only be opened with a decade of patience and a sprinkle of luck. You'd wire your $10 million commitment, accept your capital calls on a pre-determined schedule, and settle in for seven to twelve years of polite quarterly updates filled with words like "velocity," "disruption," and "pre-exit optionality." Eventually, you hoped, an exit would happen. Maybe two or three. The fund would return 3x, 5x, or, if you were really lucky, something worthy of champagne.

But that psychology has shifted. Permanently.

Today's Investors are under pressure of their own. They have to report performance to CIOs, boards, retirees, and family beneficiaries. Liquidity isn't a luxury, it's an expectation. In a world where fixed-income instruments are yielding 6%+ risk-free and inflation isn't just theoretical, locking up capital for a decade without any cash flow feels outdated, even irresponsible.

Institutional allocators are also learning from experience. They've sat through multiple funds where the paper markups were impressive, but the DPI (Distributed to Paid-In Capital) was stuck near zero for years. A portfolio full of unicorns means little when those unicorns can't find a buyer, or worse, don't have the underlying business to justify their valuations in a post-ZIRP environment.

In response, Investors have started to ask harder questions.

- When does my money come back?
- How does this model actually produce yield?
- What happens in a flat or down market?
- Can you show me cash-on-cash returns that aren't just theoretical?

These are fair questions. And increasingly, they're deal-breakers. The romance of VC-as-art-form has been replaced by the practicality of VC-as-asset-class. The best managers are responding not with defensiveness, but with redesign.

Enter the Full-Stack Venture Capital Funds™ model.

By incorporating private credit and structured income into the venture toolkit, fund managers can offer Investors a rare combination: real upside from equity investments alongside predictable yield from cash-flowing assets. The capital stack isn't just diversified across companies; it's diversified across time horizons and risk profiles. Some positions deliver quarterly interest. Others are engineered for long-term appreciation. Together, they build a portfolio that functions more like a total return fund and less like a lottery ticket.

This is not just more attractive. It's more sustainable.

A fund that pays back Investors early and often doesn't just please the CIO, it earns the right to raise the next fund on better terms. A fund that delivers yield even in flat equity markets doesn't just survive downturns, it becomes a lifeline for its Investors. And a fund that can show true capital efficiency in its deployment, recycling, and realization strategy becomes more than a blind pool; it becomes a blueprint.

This is the new psychology of smart investor capital. Less myth. More math.

Part 2: Structured Returns Without Sacrificing Upside

The old paradigm told investors they had to choose; either you get liquidity and income, or you get equity upside. Never both. That dichotomy was baked into the design of traditional venture funds' illiquid, J-curve-shaped, all-or-nothing bets.

But that tradeoff was never a law of nature. It was a limitation of imagination.

Today, smart Venture Capital models are proving you can have both: structured returns now and asymmetric upside later. The mechanism is simple but powerful: a structured credit pair with optionality.

Let's say a fund makes a $1 million interest-only loan to a post-revenue startup with solid customer retention and 70% gross margins. The company agrees to pay 13% annual interest, with quarterly payments. That cash flows immediately into the fund's income stream, fuel for investor distributions, management fees, and redeployment. But the deal doesn't stop there. Attached to the note is a warrant package for 5% equity, or the right to convert the note into preferred shares at a valuation agreed upon in advance.

That's where the upside lives.

If the company hits its stride, growing revenue, improving margins, and expanding its customer base, the fund exercises its warrants or converts its debt into equity. If the company flatlines, the fund still collects 13% annually, senior in the stack, protected by covenants and sometimes even collateral. Heads: you win. Tails: You don't lose.

This structure doesn't dilute upside; it underwrites it intelligently.

More importantly, it keeps capital productive. In a traditional venture, your dollars sit idle after deployment, waiting for a liquidity event that might be five years away. In a Full-Stack Venture Capital Funds™ model, the same capital generates income that can be recycled into new deals, creating a capital velocity rarely seen in VC.

And when structured returns are combined with dividend-paying portfolio companies, those rare but powerful ventures that kick off cash instead of burning it you begin to see a fund dynamic that resembles compounding. Early cash flow supports new investment. New investment creates new returns. Those returns are partially liquid and partially long-term, and together they drive non-linear growth in NAV and DPI.

Investors notice this. They don't have to squint at valuations and hope they're real. They can see the cash in their statements. And they don't have to choose between safety and sizzle. They get both.

This Full-Stack Venture Capital Funds™ model also disciplines fund managers. When you're targeting current income alongside long-term appreciation, you can't afford to chase hype. You need portfolio companies that are well-run, operationally sound, and monetizing a real asset. You ask harder questions in diligence. You build relationships, not just bets. And you structure your capital in a way that aligns all parties toward performance, not just paper value.

In the end, structured returns don't diminish venture. They de-risk it and strengthen it, while leaving the door open for breakouts.

It's not about replacing the 100x moonshots. It's about funding them more effectively while building a stronger base for the fund itself.

Part 3: Liquidity Without Liquidation – Smarter Cash Flow Models

One of the most persistent flaws in traditional Venture Capital is its rigid reliance on terminal events, IPOs, acquisitions, or secondaries as the only pathways to liquidity. In that model, everything is binary: a company is either illiquid or it's exited. There's no middle ground.

But in the real world, wealth is rarely built that way. In real estate, you can refinance. In private credit, you clip coupons. In private equity, you take dividends and partial recaps. Venture Capital, historically, offered none of that. It was a game of patience, speculation, and delayed gratification.

The Full-Stack Venture Capital Funds™ model changes this.

When your portfolio includes structured credit, revenue-based financing, dividend-yielding companies, and partial liquidity mechanisms, you create a system in which cash flows into the fund without liquidating the underlying equity. This is liquidity without forced exits, freedom without fire sales.

Imagine a portfolio where:

- One company pays 13% interest on a revenue-based loan, generating monthly payments.

- Another has reached steady-state profitability and issues quarterly dividends.

- A third triggers a partial secondary, in which early investors sell a fraction of their stake to new entrants at a higher valuation.

- Meanwhile, income from these sources is redeployed into new investments or returned to Investors, depending on the fund's strategy.

This dynamic creates an internal flywheel: liquidity events are happening inside the fund every quarter, without waiting for the stars to align in public markets or for strategic acquirers to show up with a premium bid.

And here's where it gets even more compelling for long-term investors: you don't need to exit your winners prematurely.

Instead of selling your best-performing companies at the first sign of a markup to meet distribution pressures, you can hold them sometimes indefinitely. Structured returns from the broader portfolio give you the breathing room. Founders aren't pushed to exit early. Investors aren't left waiting a decade for a single check. The fund becomes a true compounding vehicle, not just a waiting room for the next IPO cycle.

This approach also provides greater flexibility in managing the fund lifecycle. You can return capital to Investors early, or keep reinvesting to maximize terminal value. You can carve out mature assets into separate continuation vehicles. You can offer liquidity windows to incoming investors through NAV-based redemptions. None of this is possible in a traditional "10-year blind pool" with zero distributions until year seven.

Liquidity without liquidation isn't just a perk. It's a fundamental upgrade to how Venture Capital can operate in the modern world. It aligns with how wealth is built across other private asset classes. It makes room for patience without stagnation. And it delivers value in a form investors actually recognize: cash.

Real cash. On a real schedule. With real IRRs to match.

Part 4: Holding Through the Winner's Curve

In traditional Venture Capital, the cruel irony is that just when a company becomes truly valuable, scaling, profitable, brand-defining it's often sold. Not because the founder wants out. Not because the company has peaked. But because the VC fund investors need liquidity. The clock is ticking, the fund term is running out, and Investors are calling for returns.

So, the company exits.

Not for $1 billion when it might have hit $5 billion. Not because it's the best strategic outcome, but because it's the only way to mark the win.

BROKEN

This is the liquidation trap baked into the old Venture Capital model. The pressure to distribute often pushes funds to exit winners too early, leaving the biggest part of the value curve uncaptured.

The Full-Stack Venture Capital Funds™ model turns that trap into a choice.

By generating real income from credit and dividend-yielding assets, the fund buys itself time. It meets investor expectations along the way without being forced to sell its best-performing companies. That cash flow becomes a pressure valve, allowing the fund to hold through the winner's curve.

What's the winner's curve? It's the inflection point where a company has already de-risked major elements of product-market fit, customer acquisition, unit economics, but hasn't yet hit its exponential growth or public market potential. It's that rare window when holding longer could turn a 3x outcome into 10x, 20x, or more. But only if you can afford to wait.

In a typical fund, waiting is a luxury. In a Full-Stack Venture Capital Funds™ model, it's a design feature.

Instead of seeing exits as the only way out, you create a spectrum of outcomes:

- Strategic liquidity: Sell a small stake to new investors at higher valuations while retaining upside.

- Dividend recapitalization: Extract value without giving up ownership.

- Continuation funds: Spin off high-performers into long-dated vehicles that allow legacy Investors to exit while new ones enter.

- Permanent capital platforms: Transform evergreen holdings into yield-bearing assets that produce returns indefinitely.

The psychology of investing changes, too. When Investors receive steady distributions, they're far more patient with illiquid portions of the portfolio. When they see quarterly cash flow, they don't demand a rushed exit. They start acting more like owners and less like impatient traders.

And that's good for everyone.

Founders can think bigger and plan longer. Investors stay on for the full arc of value creation. The fund avoids the tax inefficiencies and reputation risks of selling too early. And the whole system starts to look less like a Silicon Valley casino and more like a durable engine for wealth creation.

Holding through the winner's curve is not a radical idea, it's just been hard to do until now. The Full-Stack Venture Capital Funds™ model makes it not just possible, but practical.

And when that happens, we stop asking "when do we sell?" and start asking the better question: "how far can this go?"

Part 5: Optionality at Every Stage

If the old venture model had a motto, it would be this: "Raise. Grow. Exit. Repeat." Every round was a step toward a single goal an exit typically through M&A or IPO. Optionality? That was for founders with leverage or funds with unusually patient Investors.

But in the Full-Stack Venture Capital Funds™ model, optionality isn't a luxury. It's a feature of the design.

By layering different capital instruments, credit, preferred equity, revenue-share, and common equity, a Full-Stack Venture Capital Funds™ doesn't just invest. It architects outcomes. And it does so in a way that keeps multiple doors open for both founders and investors, even as the business evolves.

Let's break it down.

Early Stage

At the earliest stage, traditional Venture Capital takes a high-risk equity bet and waits. In contrast, a Full-Stack Venture Capital Funds™ can start with small equity checks or convertible notes, then offer milestone-based follow-on capital, some of it structured. This reduces dilution early and aligns capital to progress, not just storytelling.

If a founder gains traction fast, the fund can convert its position into equity at favorable terms. If growth is slower but steady, the fund can offer revenue-based financing or asset-backed credit to bridge to the next level without a cap table explosion. Either way, the founder retains greater ownership and control, while the fund retains the optionality to participate in the next phase.

Mid Stage

Here's where traditional venture capital often forces the next round, whether the company is ready or not. But a Full-Stack Venture Capital Funds™ model has other plays.

Credit becomes a strategic tool not just as bridge financing, but as growth capital that can be repaid without equity dilution. Dividends or revenue shares start returning capital to the fund. Founders can hold off on a priced round until they've hit stronger metrics, resulting in much higher valuations and less dilution for everyone.

Want to extend the runway to profitability? Use structured credit.

Want to test a new product line without a full round? Use a working capital facility.

Want to do both, but still retain equity upside? Combine instruments.

At this stage, capital optionality becomes the founder's superpower. And the fund's risk management strategy.

Late Stage

This is where the Full-Stack model really shines.

While traditional venture funds are preparing for a sale or IPO, a Full-Stack Venture Capital Funds™ can consider:

- Selling down partial positions in secondary markets.

- Structuring recapitalizations that return cash while retaining upside.

- Converting structured positions into equity for the final leg of the journey.

- Holding indefinitely as a yield-bearing evergreen asset.

Instead of pushing for a binary outcome, the fund can optimize across return profiles, time horizons, and investor preferences.

Some Investors might want liquidity via a dividend recap or continuation vehicle.

Others might want to stay in until the very end to maximize long-term value.

The fund can accommodate both without compromising the business or the founder's vision.

This optionality matters.

Because startups don't all grow in straight lines. Because exits don't always come when it's convenient. And because value isn't always realized on someone else's schedule.

Optionality at every stage doesn't just de-risk the investment. It empowers everyone involved. It puts capital to work more intelligently. It aligns incentives over longer periods. And it removes the artificial time pressure that has plagued the venture model for decades.

In a world where adaptability wins, a Full-Stack Venture Capital Funds™ isn't just more robust. It's more humane. For founders. For investors. And for the future we're all trying to build.

Part 6: Evergreen Structures and the End of the Fund Clock

If the legacy Venture Capital model has a silent killer, it's the fund clock.

Ten years. That's the standard lifespan of a traditional venture fund. Five years to deploy capital, five years to harvest returns. The invisible countdown starts the moment the Investors wire funds. From there, it's a race to deploy, a scramble to scale, and a desperate search for exits. Not because the business is ready, but because the fund is aging out.

This model isn't just flawed, it's fundamentally misaligned with how real companies grow.

Some startups need more time. Others exit faster. Some create long-term, cash-flowing value that doesn't fit the binary IPO-or-bust playbook. But under a closed-end fund, the GP has to exit. There's no patience built into the structure.

That's where evergreen funds come in.

What Is an Evergreen Fund?

An evergreen fund is an investment vehicle with no predefined end date. It continually raises and recycles capital, reinvests proceeds, and maintains flexible liquidity mechanisms. Investors can enter or exit over time, subject to specific rules, without forcing the fund to sell assets on someone else's timeline.

In short, evergreen funds break the clock. And for Full-Stack Venture Capital Funds™, they are the ideal chassis.

Why Evergreen Works Better?

1. **Longer Holding Periods, Better Outcomes.**

   Great companies often take more than 10 years to build. A closed-end structure imposes artificial timelines, sometimes leading to premature exits or unfavorable terms. Evergreen allows the fund to hold onto winners and ride the full arc of value creation, especially in venture deals where the terminal value may be a decade or more away.

2. **Real Yield in Real Time.**

   With structured credit and income-generating investments in the portfolio, evergreen funds can generate consistent returns. These proceeds can be distributed to Investors or reinvested, providing a blend of current income and long-term appreciation. That's not just capital efficiency, it's return smoothing.

3. **Better Capital Recycling.**

   Instead of rushing to exit in year five to return capital, evergreen funds recycle interest payments, revenue shares, and early exits into new investments. That keeps the capital compounding without the costly overhead of a new fundraise every few years.

4. **Flexible Investments Onboarding and Redemption.**

   Evergreen funds allow new Investors to come in periodically at NAV or a calculated entry value, giving the fund continuous fundraising ability. Meanwhile, redemption windows offer liquidity options, so long as they're managed prudently. This gives Investors more flexibility without hurting the portfolio.

5. **Alignment with Founders.**

   Founders no longer have to scale on someone else's schedule. They can partner with a fund that grows with them, not one racing the clock. This opens up healthier conversations about profitability, dividends, buybacks, and strategic exits without the pressure of looming fund expiration dates.

The Compounding Effect Over Time

Let's rethink what a fund's lifecycle looks like with an evergreen Full-Stack Venture Capital Funds™ model:

- Year 1: Capital is deployed using structured instruments. Income begins immediately.

- Year 2: Proceeds are recycled into follow-on deals or new opportunities. Some positions convert to equity.

- Year 3–5: Distributions to Investors begin through income or partial exits. The equity portion of the portfolio starts to appreciate.

- Year 6–10: Cash-on-cash multiples grow. Investors can reinvest or redeem. High-performing venture bets reach exit velocity.

- Year 10+: The fund holds valuable equity in maturing companies, continues generating yield from credit, and compounds returns through reinvestment. New Investors enter. Older Investors may exit with realized returns. The flywheel keeps turning.

Evergreen doesn't mean stagnant. It means sustainable. It means capital that grows with opportunity, not against the clock.

A Win for Everyone

For Fund Managers, evergreen structures reduce the overhead and performance pressure of frequent fundraising.

They also allow for better long-term planning and strategic alignment.

For Investors, Evergreen provides optional liquidity, smoother returns, and longer-term exposure to truly compounding assets. Instead of a single, anxiety-ridden J-curve, they get consistent cash flow with long-duration upside.

For founders, it removes the ticking time bomb. They can optimize for value, not urgency. They can partner with truly long-term investors.

The End of the Clock Is the Beginning of Better Capital

The venture industry has spent decades pretending that innovation happens on a timer. But innovation, real, durable, transformative innovation doesn't care about a fund's vintage year. It needs capital that can flex, adapt, wait, and accelerate.

Evergreen funds give us that. And in a Full-Stack model, they unlock a kind of harmony that's been missing in Venture Capital for too long.

No more arbitrary countdowns. No more forced exits. Just better investing. Stronger partnerships. And smarter, more durable returns.

Chapter 7

Designing and Operating a Full-Stack Venture Capital Funds™

Part 1: Legal and Structural Considerations

The modern Venture Capital firm is evolving, and so too must its legal spine and structural design. Traditional fund models, blind pools with 10-year terms, vintage risk, GP/LP splits, and inflexible investment mandates were never built to accommodate the complexity and optionality of a Full-Stack Venture Capital Funds™ approach. If you're going to finance the entire journey of a company, from inception to growth to monetization, your legal chassis better be built for the whole race not just the first lap.

That's where structure becomes strategy.

One of the most misunderstood but powerful vehicles for operating a multi-asset investment strategy is the Business Development Company (BDC). Born out of the 1980 Small Business Investment Incentive Act, BDCs are a special type of closed-end investment company designed to provide capital to small and mid-sized businesses. But they do far more than that. BDCs can function like Venture Capital firms, private credit shops, and private equity investors all under one regulatory roof.

The key to the BDC structure is its ability to blend income-generating debt investments with equity upside. It allows fund managers to originate loans, collect interest, and participate in exits, all while distributing at least 90% of taxable income to investors to retain Regulated Investment Company (RIC) tax status. This makes BDCs especially attractive to investors seeking current income alongside long-term appreciation.

Compare this to a traditional venture fund, where income is almost nonexistent and all the value is locked up until an exit. Or a credit fund, which often lacks upside exposure and is limited in participating in equity rounds. The BDC structure removes these silos. It enables fund managers to flex across the capital stack, writing revenue-based loans, convertible notes, preferred equity, or taking common equity positions, all in a single vehicle.

For evergreen ambitions, you might also explore perpetual life structures or interval funds. These vehicles offer continuous capital-raising and redemption windows, enabling the fund to recycle capital and scale with investor demand. Evergreen models require robust NAV calculation and internal controls, but they unlock a different kind of investor alignment: one where the fund isn't forced to exit great companies just to meet artificial time horizons. You can hold winners longer, support portfolio companies across cycles, and manage liquidity more intelligently.

Regulatory compliance is not optional; it's foundational. Whether you operate as a BDC, RIC, LP/GP structure, or a hybrid vehicle, compliance discipline governs your ability to scale and maintain investor trust. Filing requirements, valuation standards, reporting timelines, and affiliated transaction oversight, these aren't bureaucratic chores. They're the guardrails that keep the machine running with precision and credibility.

What's often overlooked is how legal structure shapes capital formation itself. The wrong structure limits your LP base. The right one opens doors. Registered investment vehicles, for example, can access RIAs, broker-dealers, family offices, and even retail investors under certain exemptions. Meanwhile, private LP funds may appeal to institutional allocators with long-term capital but can't offer liquidity or current income. The structure is the interface between your strategy and your capital sources. Misalign that, and you'll always be fundraising uphill.

To build a Full-Stack Venture Capital Funds™, your structure must be flexible enough to accommodate the diversity of asset types, investors, and time horizons. It must allow you to operate across equity, debt, and hybrid instruments, to harvest both yield and appreciation, and to reinvest proceeds without waiting a decade for a closing bell. Done right, structure doesn't just protect you, it propels you.

Part 2: How to Underwrite Across the Stack with Rigor

If you think underwriting is just a numbers game, you're already behind. In a Full-Stack Venture Capital Funds™, underwriting is a multi-dimensional art that blends quantitative discipline with contextual wisdom. You're not just asking, "Can this company 10x?" anymore. You're also asking, "Can this company pay interest in 90 days?" and "Will this founder survive a downturn?" and "What does a downside recovery scenario really look like?"

Operating across the capital stack, credit, preferred equity, and common equity requires a sharper lens than traditional VC underwriting. In fact, it requires multiple lenses, each with its own focus and field of vision.

Let's start with credit underwriting. This is not about FICO scores and personal guarantees (although sometimes those matter too). It's about cash flow analysis, revenue durability, margin compression risk, and customer concentration. You have to be ruthless in assessing the borrower's ability to service debt, especially in pre-profit companies. Even in venture credit, where covenant-light structures are common, you still need guardrails, cash burn covenants, milestone triggers, liens on IP, and the ability to step in if the ship starts to sink.

Then there's convertible and preferred equity underwriting, which sits in the gray zone between debt and common equity. This is where structure becomes your best friend.

You're pricing not just risk, but optionality rights to participate in future rounds, liquidation preferences, board seats, warrants, and information rights. You're building your return not just on outcomes, but on timing and control. The math gets murky here, and the models have to stretch: scenario analysis, option pricing theory, and cap table forecasting all in a single workbook.

And of course, we have common equity. This is the classic venture lens: big markets, bold founders, competitive moats, traction milestones, and the ever-elusive product-market fit. But in a Full-Stack Venture Capital Funds™ context, you underwrite common equity not in isolation, but as part of a broader portfolio mosaic. That bold Series A check might sit beside a revenue-based loan and a piece of preferred equity, all in the same company. The question becomes: how do these positions interact under different scenarios? How do you protect the floor while leaving the ceiling uncapped?

Underwriting across the stack demands discipline, but also empathy. It requires understanding how founders operate under pressure, how markets respond to macro shocks, and how your capital actually affects the business. A good underwriter in this world isn't just a spreadsheet samurai. They're a psychologist, a risk engineer, and a tactician.

One of the most overlooked tools in Full-Stack Venture Capital Funds™ underwriting is cross-scenario stress testing. What happens if the company misses revenue by 30%? What if they raise a down round in 18 months? What if interest rates spike and the cost of debt doubles? These aren't theoretical exercises. They're predictive frameworks that prepare you for what's next and help you build capital structures that adapt rather than crack.

You also need to deal with pacing discipline. With more instruments at your disposal, it becomes tempting to "do something" just because you can. But writing a convertible note when equity isn't justified, or extending a credit facility to a company with no plan to repay, is not optionality, it's negligence. Underwriting in a Full-Stack Venture Capital Funds™ is not about doing more deals. It's about doing smarter deals, with the right tools at the right time for the right companies.

Finally, Full-Stack Venture Capital Funds™ underwriting means being brutally honest with yourself about where your returns are coming from. Are you relying too heavily on one form of capital to carry the fund? Are you exposing your Investors to hidden risks by stacking on risky instruments? Great firms build systems that make these patterns visible early and course-correct before it's too late.

In this game, rigor isn't just about saying "no" to bad deals. It's about saying "yes" in the smartest possible way.

Part 3: Governance, Valuation, and Cross-Asset Due Diligence

In a Full-Stack Venture Capital Funds™ model, governance is not a formality it's the operating system. When you invest across asset classes, you introduce complexity. And complexity, unmanaged, is chaos. Good governance makes sure the fund doesn't just survive that complexity but uses it to gain an advantage.

Start with the board. Not every investment will come with a seat at the table, but when it does, you need to be prepared to help govern with clarity and consistency. If you've extended credit, you're not just a lender, you're a stakeholder with downside exposure. If you've taken equity, you're not just a cheerleader, you're a long-term capital partner responsible for oversight. In Full-Stack Venture Capital Funds™ models, governance needs to flex with your position: sometimes active, sometimes passive, but always engaged.

Then there's valuation. This is where most Full-Stack Venture Capital Funds™ can stub their toe. Venture equity is notoriously hard to value, and private credit adds its own layers of complexity discount rates, prepayment assumptions, and recovery models. Add in preferred shares, warrants, convertible notes, and revenue-based financing, and suddenly your portfolio accounting system looks like it was built by Rube Goldberg.

You need a valuation framework that's consistent, auditable, and defensible. Not just for Investors and auditors, but for yourself. Because if you don't understand what your portfolio is worth and why you can't make rational decisions about follow-on investments, fund performance, or manager compensation. In a Full-Stack Venture Capital Funds™ world, valuation isn't an annual fire drill. It's a living, breathing discipline.

That brings us to cross-asset due diligence. In a traditional VC fund, diligence focuses on market size, founder capability, tech defensibility, and growth potential. In a credit fund, diligence zooms in on balance sheets, receivables, revenue quality, and default risk. In private equity, it's all about control, margins, operating leverage, and exit optionality.

But what happens when your fund does all three? You can't silo diligence into separate boxes anymore. You need to create a diligence model that integrates across dimensions.

You're no longer just asking, "Is this a good company?" You're asking, "Which instrument fits this company at this time, and what are the risks and returns across each?"

This is where a Full-Stack Venture Capital Funds™ diligence path comes into play. While I will provide more information about my company in the Epilogue at the end of this book, it is worth noting that at my firm, Capital Q˚ Ventures, we've used a multi-tiered approach that incorporates both quantitative and qualitative analysis of prospective portfolio companies. First, a universal filter: is it a vision of the future we can support, is this company mission-fit, with honest and talented leaders, and in a space we understand? Then a stack-specific module: is this a credit opportunity, an equity play, or a hybrid deal? Then a risk-overlay: how does this position interact with the rest of the fund's exposure?

GOVERNANCE AND CROSS-ASSET DUE DILIGENCE FRAMEWORK

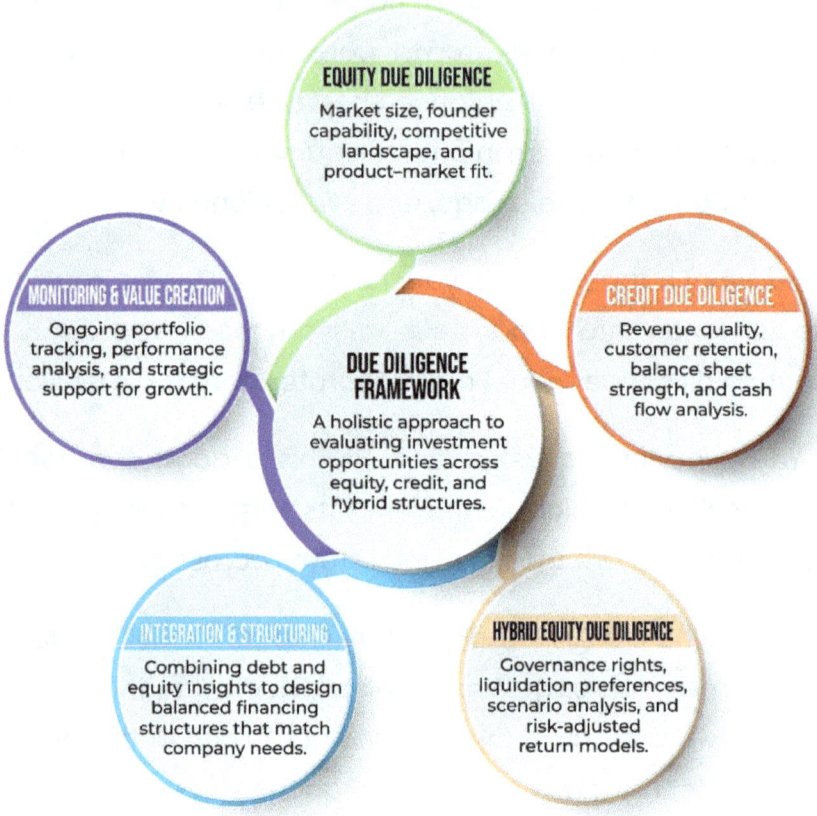

A holistic diligence model that evaluates opportunities across equity, credit, and hybrid instruments.

One founder might need a $1.5 million loan today and a $3 million Series A in 12 months. You need due diligence on that whole journey upfront. You're underwriting not just to the next mile marker, but to the whole map. It's not about placing a bet, it's about buying an option and preparing for every possible turn.

Strong due diligence in a Full-Stack Venture Capital Funds™ is both broad and deep. It's checking customer contracts for churn clauses. It's calling references for founders you might lend to before you invest in. It's reviewing IP filings, but also diving into cost of goods sold on a per-unit basis. It's talking to customers, partners, competitors, ex-employees, and sometimes even ex-investors.

It's also knowing when you're out of your depth and bringing in specialists who aren't. A Full-Stack Venture Capital Funds™ should be humble enough to know when a vertical is too foreign, and disciplined enough to say no when the risk-reward tradeoff just isn't there. Great governance isn't just oversight, it's self-awareness in action.

All of this comes together in one final word: integrity. Because in a complex capital stack, the temptation to game the system, overvalue an investment, overlook a red flag, push a deal through because "we already spent time on it" is very real. But a Full-Stack Venture Capital Funds™ built to last must be built on trust, both internally and externally.

If your internal processes can't survive a flashlight, you've already lost. Good governance shines the flashlight early, often, and without apology.

Part 4: Building Internal Teams to Support Diverse Capital Tools

If the traditional Venture Capital model is a sleek two-seater sports car built for speed, not luggage, the Full-Stack Venture Capital Funds™ is a high-performance utility vehicle. It has to go fast, sure, but it also needs to haul cargo, endure long stretches, and switch terrain without throwing a rod. And that means you don't just need a driver. You need a pit crew, a mechanic, a logistics team, and someone to scout the route ahead.

KEY TEAMS & COLLABORATION STRUCTURE

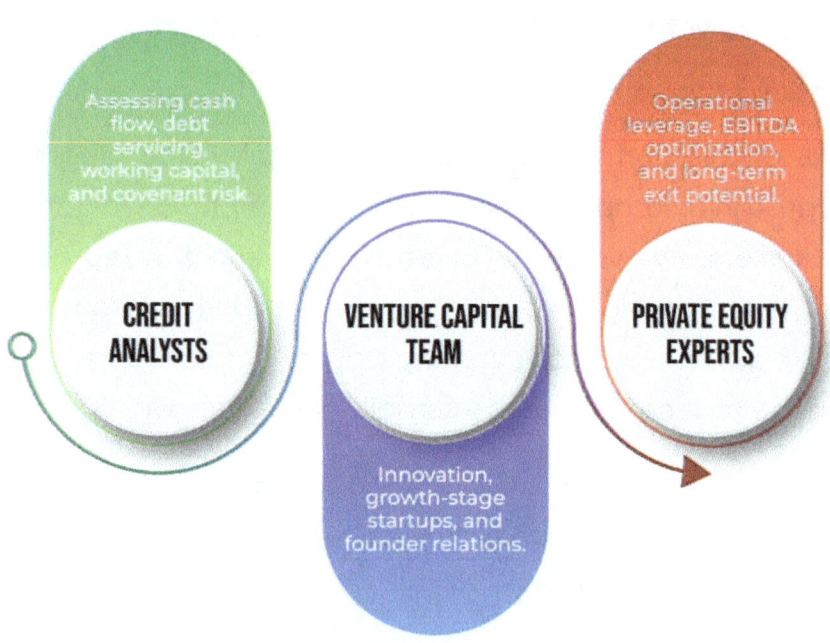

Assessing cash flow, debt servicing, working capital, and covenant risk.

Operational leverage, EBITDA optimization, and long-term exit potential.

CREDIT ANALYSTS

VENTURE CAPITAL TEAM

PRIVATE EQUITY EXPERTS

Innovation, growth-stage startups, and founder relations.

The integrated collaboration model between Venture Capital teams, Credit Analysts, and Private Equity experts, each contributing discipline-specific insights to operate a Full-Stack Venture Capital Funds™

Operating across venture, credit, and private equity means building an internal team with different muscles. You need Venture Capital team members who understand early-stage innovation and founder psychology. You need credit analysts who can assess balance sheets, calculate covenant risk, and understand working capital cycles. And you need private equity pros who think in terms of EBITDA margins, control provisions, and exit scenarios. All these people need to speak a common language with capital fluency, but they also need to bring unique perspectives to the table.

The hardest part? Avoiding silos.

In traditional firms, teams often specialize vertically. The credit team does its thing. The venture folks handle startups. The PE guys look down on everyone else from their spreadsheet mountain. But in a Full-Stack Venture Capital Funds™ model, isolation kills synergy. Instead, you need a horizontal culture of collaboration where a venture associate can pull in a credit lead to ask, "Is this bridge loan priced right?" Or a private equity partner can tap the venture scout to say, "Do you believe this founder can scale past Series C?"

Cross-functional communication must be designed into the system, not just hoped for. That means weekly portfolio reviews where everyone hears about every deal. It means integrated CRM systems, so deal notes aren't trapped in personal files. It means shared diligence frameworks where risk is assessed through a common lens. And it means compensation structures that reward collective outcomes rather than territorial wins.

You also need strong middle and back-office support. Full-Stack Venture Capital Funds™ investing introduces complexity in fund accounting, compliance, valuation tracking, and investor communications. You'll need a rock-solid CFO or at least a third-party administrator who thinks like one. Your legal counsel must understand how to paper venture equity, draft credit agreements, and navigate hybrid instruments without slowing you down or exposing the fund. And your reporting tools must allow for apples-to-apples comparison across investments that look nothing alike.

When we started, we quickly learned that no single person could cover the entire capital stack. Instead, we built our bench intentionally. Our credit team includes people who've worked in private debt and commercial banking. Our venture team includes founders who've raised capital and operators who've scaled companies. And we began by relying on fractional or part-time specialists, valuation consultants, CFOs-for-hire, sector-specific experts who drop in at key points to sharpen our edge without bloating our cost structure.

Hiring for curiosity is just as important as hiring for credentials. A great Venture Capital investor may not know how to build a loan amortization schedule, but if they're curious and collaborative, they'll sit down with the credit lead and learn what levers matter. Likewise, a credit analyst who's only worked with mature companies may need to get comfortable with startup chaos, but if they bring rigor and humility, they'll grow into the role.

Finally, don't forget culture. The best multi-asset firms cultivate a shared mission. Not just to make money, but to solve the capital inefficiencies that hold great companies back. Your team must believe that better capital models build better businesses. That founders deserve capital partners, not predators. That investors deserve outcomes, not optics. When that belief takes root, job titles fade, and collaboration becomes the default.

To paraphrase Peter Drucker: culture eats structure for breakfast. But in this case, you need both. A culture that celebrates diverse perspectives and a structure that enables those perspectives to work together in real time.

So yes, Full-Stack Venture Capital Funds™ investing is more complex. But when your team is aligned, integrated, and fluent across instruments, it doesn't feel harder. It feels like flying with both wings.

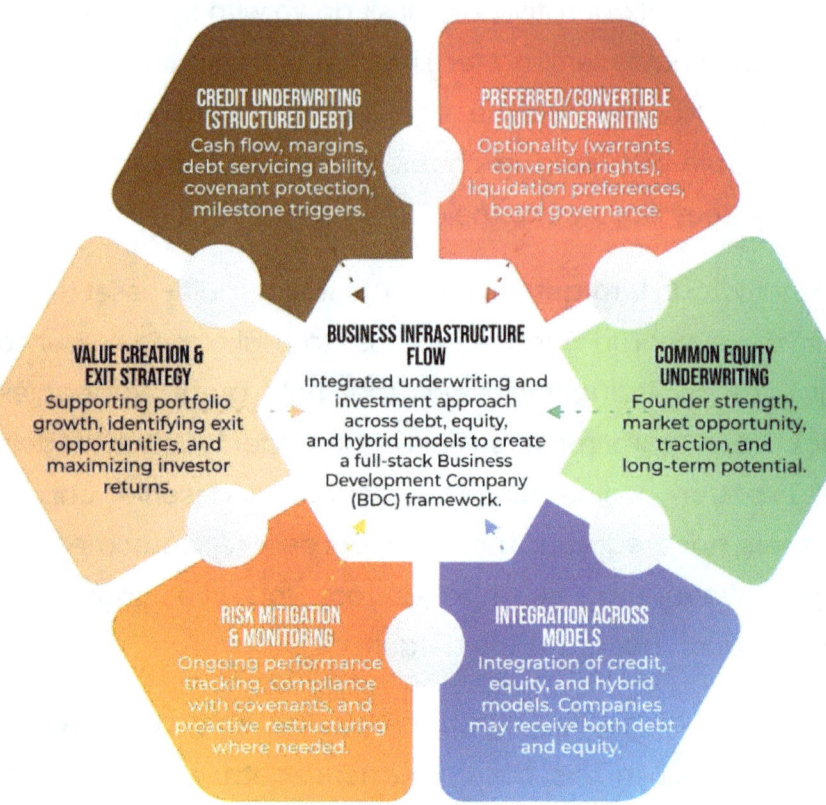

The integrated business infrastructure flow of a Full-Stack BDC, linking debt, preferred equity, common equity, hybrid structures, risk monitoring, and exit strategy into a unified underwriting and operating system.

Chapter 8

Better for Communities – Local Wealth, Real Impact

For decades, Venture Capital has been largely indifferent to geography. Silicon Valley taught the world that innovation was an exportable commodity, and capital chased talent wherever the buzz was loudest, not where the roots were deepest. Founders were encouraged to move. Ecosystems were measured by unicorns. And the phrase "impact investing" was often treated as code for concessionary returns.

But what if we've had it backwards?

What if the most enduring impact comes not from capital that flies in and flies out but from capital that stays?

A Full-Stack Venture Capital Funds™ model isn't just better for fund returns and founders. It's also better for communities. And not in a vague, feel-good, PR-campaign kind of way. We're talking about structural, measurable, regenerative impact, the kind that anchors talent, grows local wealth, and recycles prosperity over decades, not funding cycles.

Wealth That Stays Local

Traditional venture models often extract more than they leave behind. When capital comes from coastal Investors and exits end in acquisitions by multinational tech firms, the financial upside vanishes from the local community. The founders may win. The investors may win. But the city or region that nurtured the idea gets little more than a press release and a few short-lived jobs.

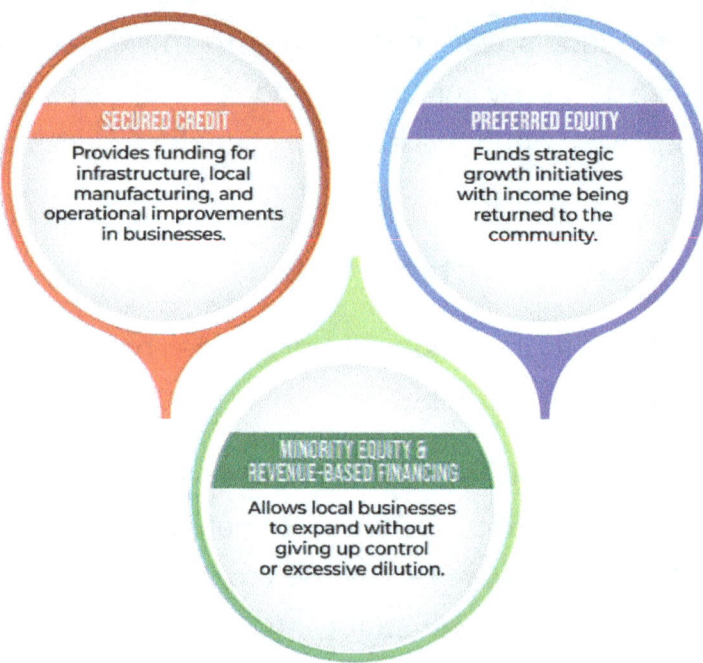

CAPITAL STACK FOR COMMUNITY DEVELOPMENT: COMPREHENSIVE INVESTMENT STRATEGY

SECURED CREDIT
Provides funding for infrastructure, local manufacturing, and operational improvements in businesses.

PREFERRED EQUITY
Funds strategic growth initiatives with income being returned to the community.

MINORITY EQUITY & REVENUE-BASED FINANCING
Allows local businesses to expand without giving up control or excessive dilution.

A visual overview of how secured credit, preferred equity, and minority equity/revenue-based financing work together to fund local businesses, strengthen regional infrastructure, and keep wealth circulating within communities.

A Full-Stack Venture Capital Funds™, multi-asset model challenges this pattern by focusing on long-term participation in the companies it backs, not just exit multiples. Income-generating credit structures and dividend strategies mean that money comes back into the fund continuously. Those proceeds can then be redeployed into other local companies, creating a virtuous cycle of reinvestment.

In evergreen structures, the compounding effect is even more powerful. Gains from one local success story can help fund the next one. A community's economic base isn't eroded by success; it's amplified by it.

Job Creation with Staying Power

Equity-fueled blitzscaling can create jobs fast, but they're often fragile. When capital dries up or the next round doesn't materialize, companies slash headcounts, close offices, or pivot away from their original communities.

Full-Stack Venture Capital Funds™ are more deliberate. Their capital structure allows for right-sized growth, not just rapid growth. That's critical for sustainable job creation. When a company grows with revenue-based financing, structured credit, and responsible equity, it tends to scale in proportion to its fundamentals. The result? Fewer flash-in-the-pan hiring binges, and more long-term employment tied to a real business model.

In this way, community-focused Venture Capital becomes economic development, not just capital deployment.

Infrastructure and Institutions, Not Just Startups

Another powerful feature of the multi-asset model is that it isn't limited to high-growth software plays. It can fund local manufacturing, logistics, education platforms, healthcare services, and brick-and-mortar businesses that generate stable income and community utility even if they don't generate 100x exits.

Traditional VCs often pass on these opportunities. But with structured credit and private equity-style investment tools in the arsenal, these companies become viable investments. The fund can generate income. The community gains services. And the founders don't have to warp their business model into something unrecognizable just to get funded.

In time, this supports the growth of local entrepreneurial ecosystems that are more than pitch competitions and accelerators. We're talking about schools that teach capital literacy. Apprenticeships that train workers for new industries. Civic partnerships that align local policy with economic inclusion. A catalyst of local resilience.

Entrepreneurial Mobility and Inclusion as Economic Justice

We've all heard the tired stats. Venture Capital is still disproportionately allocated to founders in a few zip codes, with Ivy League degrees and networks that trace back to

Sand Hill Road. Less than 2% of Venture Capital dollars go to women. Even fewer go to Black and Latino founders. And despite years of headlines calling for change, the needle barely moves.

The problem isn't intent. It is structure.

Traditional VC is built on scarcity, velocity, and exits. Firms raise large pools of capital, pressure founders to grow quickly, and rely on a small number of outsized wins to justify the rest. In this framework, investing in underestimated founders or in regions without massive startup ecosystems is seen as "risky." The system pretends to be meritocratic, but it favors the familiar.

A Full-Stack Venture Capital Funds™ model breaks this cycle.

By offering a broader spectrum of capital tools, debt, revenue-based financing, strategic equity, and long-duration hold options, firms can fund a wider range of businesses run by a more diverse set of people. You don't need every company to be a billion-dollar exit to make the math work. You need consistent, intelligent capital deployment and strong relationships with operators who know their markets.

When capital becomes more flexible, it becomes more inclusive.

Let's take an example.

A third-generation family business in a mid-sized city has an opportunity to expand. They don't want to give up control, nor do they have the traction to raise a Series A. But their cash flows are stable. A Full-Stack Venture Capital Funds™ can step in with structured credit or minority equity. The company grows. Jobs are created. Ownership remains intact. And the community wins.

That same model can apply to overlooked tech founders, solo entrepreneurs, immigrant-owned businesses, or first-time founders who don't speak the language of VC decks but know how to build and sell.

This is not philanthropy. It's intelligent underwriting. When done right, it generates real financial and societal returns. And over time, it helps democratize the startup economy.

Instead of just funding the top 1% of founders, we can fund the 99% with 1% discipline.

The Multiplier Effect of Local Anchoring

When capital lands in a coastal megafund, it often disappears into a pipeline of San Francisco term sheets, New York boardrooms, and exit headlines that never touch the ground where most people live. But when capital is anchored locally, when it's deployed in businesses that operate within and serve real communities, the effect is not linear. It's exponential.

Here's what I mean: When you invest in a local business, you're not just investing in one company. You're investing in a local accountant, a local landlord, a local marketing agency, a local payroll clerk, and dozens of other economic actors that depend on that business's growth and stability. And when that business expands? The ripple effect kicks in.

Those secondary businesses hire. Those hires spend locally. Property values inch up. Tax revenues increase. Civic investment becomes more viable. Your one check, strategically placed, becomes a lever that lifts an entire block, sometimes an entire town.

Compare that to a traditional VC-backed startup in a coastal city. Even if it's a roaring success, where do the gains go? Investors split the return. Founders might move up the Peninsula or into a Manhattan brownstone. A few employees get payouts. But what's the local economic multiplier? It's thin. That capital could have just as easily been printed in a server farm in Delaware.

Local anchoring also protects against the all-eggs-in-one-basket syndrome. When multi-asset funds engage with portfolio companies across credit, equity, and even joint ventures, they develop deep roots with businesses, not just shallow touchpoints.

These are not just investments. They become relationships embedded in a place.

And while big cities will always play a role in innovation, the next wave of American wealth creation may very well emerge from regions long ignored by the Sand Hill playbook. If you want real resilience, economic, social, and cultural, you have to build in layers, not just in leaps.

Wealth that stays local doesn't just create returns. It creates legacy.

From Transactional to Transformational Capital

In traditional Venture Capital, capital is transactional by design. A check is written, a stake is taken, and a time clock starts ticking toward an exit. The relationship, while cordial, is governed by math: multiple on invested capital, internal rate of return, and the mythical "10x." It's deal-first, founder-second, and community rarely even enters the equation.

But Full-Stack Venture Capital Funds™ is transformational capital? That plays a different game.

Transformational capital isn't just about multiplying dollars; it's about compounding impact. Not in a fluffy, mission-statement kind of way, but in tangible, measurable effects: job creation, infrastructure development, business longevity, and economic mobility.

When a Full-Stack Venture Capital Funds™ engages with a company through credit, equity, and operational support, it's not just betting on a product. It's betting on a platform for change. That business becomes a vehicle for more than just shareholder value. It becomes a center of gravity for a local ecosystem.

Here's a real-world illustration: Suppose you lend $500,000 to a small but promising regional manufacturing company. That money allows them to hire 10 more employees, double output, and negotiate better terms for raw materials. As the business stabilizes, the same fund takes a small equity stake, helping them modernize operations and enter new markets. Over time, the company expands its facility, trains dozens of new workers, and becomes the go-to employer in the county.

That's not just an investment. That's a transformation of local economic infrastructure.

And because the fund has aligned interests across the stack, not just as a shareholder, but also as a lender and long-term strategic partner, the incentives are structured to prioritize sustainable growth over hype-driven scale.

Full-Stack Venture Capital Funds™ aren't building portfolios. They're building economic foundations.

In a time when many communities feel economically abandoned or hollowed out by globalization and technological displacement, this model offers something rare: proximity with purpose.

It says, "We're here with you. We're not just betting on your zip code. We're investing in your future."

Community Wealth as an Investment Strategy

Let's put this plainly: capital has a home address. It either stays and compounds where it's deployed, or it gets extracted and whisked away to anonymous Investors and global banks that couldn't find your town on a map.

Traditional venture funds are, by design, extractive. They hunt for returns in early-stage businesses, hope for an outsized exit, and move on. Any positive community impact is usually accidental or a happy byproduct of scale. And when those companies do make it big? The benefits often bypass the neighborhoods where the real work happened. The headquarters have been moved. Jobs get offshored. Equity gains get consolidated.

Multi-asset funds challenge this gravitational pull by design. They create a system where wealth is not just generated, it's retained and reinvested locally.

Here's how:

- Dividend-Paying Structures: By including credit or preferred equity instruments that return current income, funds can pay out distributions without requiring a liquidation event. That income doesn't just go to institutions. It goes to local co-investors, employee ESOPs, community banks, and municipal pension plans. In other words, people with skin in the local game.

- Local Co-Investment Opportunities: These funds can invite regional stakeholders successful entrepreneurs, foundations, and family offices to participate alongside them in deals. This democratizes access and creates shared wins that tie local fortunes to business success in a very real, bank-account-reflecting way.

- Evergreen Structures: Rather than rushing toward exit at all costs, evergreen vehicles can hold onto high-performing local companies, giving them room to grow sustainably. This preserves jobs, strengthens communities, and keeps institutional memory and tax revenue where it belongs.

- Capacity Building: Multi-asset funds often roll up their sleeves. They help build accounting systems, professionalize operations, and connect founders to national distribution or government contracts. These investments in capacity don't just help one company. They strengthen the entire regional entrepreneurial infrastructure.

There's something revolutionary about this: using sophisticated capital tools not just to extract value, but to embed it. To say, "Our returns don't come from your community. They come with your community."

In this way, the Full-Stack Venture Capital Funds™ model becomes a tool for strategic economic empowerment. Not a subsidy. Not charity. Just smart investing that actually rewards proximity and commitment.

Because when capital shows up consistently, with patience and partnership, communities do more than survive.

They start to thrive.

The Local Multiplier Effect: It's Not Just Theory

If you've ever sat in an economic development meeting, you've heard the term "local multiplier effect" tossed around like confetti. The theory is simple: when a dollar is spent at a local business, it recirculates through wages, purchases, and community services, amplifying its impact. A dollar spent at the farmer's market buys lunch at the taco stand, which pays the plumber, who hires a graphic designer, all within a 10-mile radius.

Now imagine replacing that single consumer dollar with institutional investment capital. Not just into one startup, but through a fund that invests across credit, equity, and growth-stage companies, all rooted in the region.

That's not just a multiplier.

That's an economic windfall.

Here's what it looks like in practice:

- A fund makes a revenue-based loan to a local manufacturer upgrading equipment. The repayment comes out of new sales revenue, not equity. The manufacturer adds three shifts and hires from the local workforce.

- That same fund takes an equity stake in a logistics software company across town. The company grows, signs the manufacturer as a client, and needs to expand office space.

- A line of credit is extended to a community grocer serving low-income neighborhoods. Inventory turns faster, supplier discounts are negotiated, and margins improve.

- A portion of fund profits is reinvested through a regional development initiative that supports job training, STEM education, and broadband infrastructure.

Each move reinforces the others. Jobs beget tax base. Success stories beget more founders. Reliable returns beget more capital.

And because the fund isn't built solely around unicorn-or-bust venture bets, the cycle doesn't require billion-dollar exits to sustain itself. It thrives on repeatable wins, risk-adjusted capital, and patient stewardship.

The most powerful part?

These aren't charity cases. These are commercially viable companies, gritty, inventive, and often overlooked, whose biggest challenge is not product-market fit but capital-market mismatch. By bringing the right blend of tools, a Full-

Stack Venture Capital Funds™ serves as both a financier and a force multiplier.

Communities don't need more handouts.

They need alignment. And when capital is structured to win when the community wins, magic happens. Not theoretical. Not abstract. But tangible, compoundable, and scalable.

Who Gets the Carried Interest?

In traditional VC, carried interest, the performance-based share of fund profits flows to the general partners. These are the fund managers, the rainmakers, the spreadsheet slayers. And to be clear, they earn it. Raising capital, sourcing deals, coaching founders, wrangling Investors, it's no small feat. But in the old model, carried interest feels like a one-way street. The community that houses the startup, educates the workforce, builds the infrastructure, and provides the customer base? They're watching the exits from the sidewalk.

What if interest became a shared prosperity tool, rather than just a reward for fund managers?

That's not a socialist fever dream. It's smart capitalism.

Some funds, the ones thinking bigger, are already doing this in early forms:

- Community carry pools where a portion of performance fees are redirected into nonprofit funds for housing, education, or economic development.

- Employee carry programs that extend upside not just to the founding team, but to line-level workers at portfolio companies.

- Founder pledge models, where entrepreneurs commit a slice of their gains to regional reinvestment or philanthropic initiatives.

It's not about diluting incentives, it's about broadening them.

Because here's the uncomfortable truth: if only the cap table wins, we've failed. When a liquidity event creates a paper millionaire, but the neighborhood around the startup office sees no material improvement, we've lost the plot.

Contrast that with a model where capital circulates. Where each successful exit seeds the next fund. Where management fees help build job training programs. Where local stakeholders, schools, nonprofits, and chambers of commerce are aligned with fund performance, not just spectators.

In that model, carried interest is still carried, but it's also shared.

The math still works. In fact, it works better. Investors like seeing systemic impact. Founders like joining a mission. Communities like having a seat at the table. And the firm? It attracts better deals, deeper roots, and long-term relevance.

This isn't theoretical. It's starting to happen.

And the firms that adopt it early won't just outperform, they'll outlast.

The Invisible Impact of Employee Retention

There's a silent hemorrhage happening inside most startups, and it rarely shows up on the pitch deck.

It's not burn rate. It's not CAC. It's not even churn.

It's a talent drain. And it's crushing.

Every time a trained, committed employee walks out the door, they take with them institutional memory, customer relationships, technical fluency, and team cohesion. Multiply that across an early-stage team, and the cost is existential.

Now, ask yourself: how often do traditional venture firms factor employee retention into their capital models?

Almost never.

They invest in code, IP, and charisma but not culture. They'll fund a marketing budget before a professional development stipend. They'll pay for a $25,000 rebrand, but not a $2,500 mental health benefit.

And yet, the most reliable predictor of long-term success in a startup isn't brilliance, it's stability.

Full-Stack Venture Capital Funds™, on the other hand, are uniquely positioned to interrupt the turnover cycle. Here's how:

- Credit-based capital can provide an operational cushion, reducing the pressure to cut staff during fundraising valleys.

- Longer hold periods and evergreen structures create internal continuity, helping founders invest in training rather than just talent acquisition.

- Flexible financing tools allow companies to design retention programs, phantom equity, and milestone bonuses, as well as professional growth pathways that don't require diluting ownership at the seed stage.

When the capital stack aligns with the business journey, people stop being expendable line items and become long-term collaborators. And that shift changes everything.

Founders build deeper teams. Employees think like owners. Communities see companies as employers, not just tenants.

It may not show up in a Series A press release. But over time, those retained employees, the ones who stay through thick and thin, are the ones who build the real value.

Because code gets rewritten. Products pivot. Markets change.

But people? People are the compounding asset.

And any fund that doesn't design for that isn't investing, it's speculating.

Financing the Local Multiplier Effect

You've probably heard the old line: "A dollar spent locally circulates seven times before it leaves the community." It's catchy and largely true. Economists call it the local multiplier effect, and for all the models and metrics in our industry, this simple idea often gets left behind.

Traditional Venture Capital doesn't just ignore it; it actively extracts from it.

Think about the typical lifecycle of a venture-backed startup. Founders raise in San Francisco or New York. The money comes from institutional Investors based in Boston, Zurich, or Singapore. The startup builds somewhere cheap, maybe Austin or Tampa. Then, if they're lucky, they exit via an IPO or an acquisition, and the lion's share of the return flows right back to the coasts or overseas.

The community that hosted the startup? Provided the workforce? Supplied the office space, the baristas, the accountants, and the childcare?

They get applause, not participation.

Now flip the model. A Full-Stack Venture Capital Funds™, dividend-oriented, locally anchored fund does a few things differently.

- It can deploy private credit to support startup operations and commercial real estate development in tandem, keeping both jobs and rent in the community.

- It can issue equity with long-hold flexibility, enabling company HQs to stay rooted locally rather than chasing IPO dreams in big markets.

- It can prioritize cashflow-positive ventures that feed earnings back into the fund and thus into Investors who often live in the same ZIP code.

Suddenly, that dollar doesn't just circle. It builds. The CFO hires a local accountant. The CEO buys a house down the street. The marketing team hosts an event that fills restaurants and books hotel rooms. The company donates to the neighborhood school.

Over time, these aren't just companies. They're community institutions not because they have to be, but because the capital model made it possible.

And here's the best part: this isn't charity. It's just good economics.

When a founder knows their investors are part of the town, the region, the story they build differently. They hire with care. They think long-term. They make decisions rooted in place, not just price.

And in doing so, they reinforce the very fabric of the place they call home.

That's not a side effect. That's a design feature.

B R O K E N

Blending Capital with Civic Infrastructure

Walk through any revitalized downtown corridor, a place that ten years ago was boarded up but now boasts indie coffee shops, co-working spaces, and tech startups tucked between historic buildings, and you'll notice something. These places weren't rebuilt solely with government grants. Nor were they born from pure philanthropy.

They were financed, often quietly, by private capital that had civic IQ investors who understood that infrastructure is more than roads and bridges. It's also broadband, logistics, childcare, workforce training, and trust.

The most effective Full-Stack Venture Capital Funds™ firms don't just write checks. They act as anchor tenants in the local economic story.

Here's how this plays out in the real world:

- A fund backs a promising logistics startup, but instead of just funding software, it also finances the warehouse buildout, leases it to the company, and later refinances it with permanent debt.

- It invests in a healthcare venture, then pairs it with a credit facility to fund a local clinic expansion that uses the startup's product, creating both adoption and a stronger local healthcare network.

- A growing employer needs talent. The fund co-sponsors a training program with the local community college, builds a pipeline, and shares upside with those who complete the program and stay on board.

That's the civic flywheel.

The returns? Still there. Still strong. But now they show up in multiple P&Ls, not just the fund's internal rate of return, but also in rising median wages, growing tax bases, improved public services, and neighborhood resilience.

This is not impact investing in the traditional, check-the-box sense. It's not charity wrapped in finance. It's finance at its smartest, recognizing that healthy communities are alpha generators in the long run.

In this model, capital is not just present. It's embedded.

And once you see what that kind of embedded capital can do, how it can help de-risk early ventures, accelerate adoption, retain talent, and grow enterprise value from the inside out, it's hard to go back to passive LP structures that do little more than chase markups on paper.

The civic layer is no longer optional. It's the connective tissue that turns portfolios into ecosystems.

LOCAL ECONOMIC MULTIPLIER EFFECT: REINVESTMENT IN LOCAL COMMUNITIES

A visual depiction of how investment in local businesses drives job creation, reinvestment, and compounding economic growth within communities.

And ecosystems, unlike portfolios, can survive and thrive through volatility.

B R O K E N
From Wealth Extraction to Wealth Circulation

The traditional Venture Capital model has long followed a predictable playbook: invest early, grow fast, exit big, and return capital to Investors, most of whom are geographically and emotionally distant from the places where that value was actually created.

It's a model optimized for wealth extraction. Pull capital from local economies, concentrate it in high-growth companies, and eventually cash out into global financial markets.

But there's a problem with that cycle. When the capital exits, so does the energy. Local economies are left hollowed out, temporary hosts to companies that used their infrastructure, their people, and their goodwill, only to relocate post-acquisition or post-IPO to a more "efficient" headquarters somewhere else.

This isn't just a bad outcome for communities. It's an increasingly fragile model for investors, too. Chasing growth in disconnected silos leaves funds vulnerable to macro headwinds, frothy valuations, and limited control over exit outcomes.

Full-Stack Venture Capital Funds™, however, offers an alternative. One that's rooted in wealth circulation rather than extraction.

Here's what that looks like in practice:

- When you use structured credit instead of pure equity, you can return capital to investors while keeping companies grounded in their home markets.

- When you finance both the startup and its supporting supply chain, you create sticky growth, the kind that doesn't immediately relocate at the first acquisition offer.

- When founders grow with less dilution and more optionality, they're less likely to flip their company for a quick win and more likely to build something enduring in their own backyard.

This is not just about building better companies. It's about building better economies, ones where local capital, local talent, and local returns form a self-reinforcing loop.

When done right, these loops can last generations.

They support the entrepreneur opening a second facility in her hometown. The developer is rehabbing Main Street buildings for a new wave of businesses. The teacher whose pension fund holds a piece of a local BDC that's quietly compounding returns while funding ventures her students might one day work for.

Wealth circulation isn't soft. It's durable.

It doesn't appear in a single mega-exit. It shows up in a thousand economic nodes, lighting up in concert: jobs created, taxes paid, real estate stabilized, and regional confidence restored.

In this world, the fund is no longer an outsider. It's a keystone species in the local economy.

And when the ecosystem thrives, so does the fund.

A Capital Stack for the Community, Not Just the Company

In traditional Venture Capital, the capital stack is narrowly designed. It's engineered for the company and specifically for the investors in that company. It's optimized to maximize the internal rate of return, not shared prosperity. But what if the capital stack could be designed with the entire community in mind?

This doesn't mean giving up return expectations or inserting soft capital out of obligation. It means broadening the aperture of what strategic capital can do.

Take a Full-Stack Venture Capital Funds™ operating in a regional market. Instead of simply writing a seed equity check to a high-growth startup and waiting seven years for an exit, that fund could:

- Offer a secured credit facility to a family-owned warehouse that will serve as the startup's distribution hub

- Make a preferred equity investment in the co-manufacturing facility, expanding operations to fulfill the startup's demand

- Fund a leasehold improvement loan to help the startup open a community-facing retail space

These are not side bets. These are core components of the startup's operating success and the fund's integrated return strategy.

Even more critically, these structures create multiple access points for community participation. Credit unions, regional banks, local pension plans, and even community foundations can syndicate into these tranches. Instead of being boxed out of early-stage innovation, they're brought in on terms that match their risk tolerance and liquidity needs.

The capital stack becomes a bridge between innovation and inclusion.

Done well, this approach turns every investment into a node of economic density, concentrating jobs, infrastructure, and downstream activity in the same geography where the company is growing.

And it builds a stronger flywheel. Because when your portfolio companies are embedded in a healthy ecosystem, they attract better talent, generate more goodwill, and often achieve higher valuations. Not despite their location, but because of it.

This is how a fund becomes not just a financier, but a force multiplier.

It doesn't happen by chance. It happens by design.

And it starts with a new philosophy: the full capital stack should serve not just the cap table, but the community.

Unlocking the Power of Regional Ecosystems

Silicon Valley taught us a lot about concentration. About the gravitational pull of capital and the network effects of proximity. But what it didn't teach us, at least not intentionally, was what happens when you extract more than you invest in the region.

In San Francisco, the rise of unicorns didn't translate into more affordable housing. Or better infrastructure. Or a broad-based opportunity. The wealth gap widened. Communities fractured. The talent pool got priced out of its own backyard.

That's not a model to replicate. It's a warning.

Now consider the inverse. Imagine what happens when a venture ecosystem is intentionally rooted in the region it serves. Not just headquartered there, but genuinely interdependent with the surrounding economy.

It starts with visibility. Local founders see other local founders succeed. College students interning at tech startups. Community colleges teaching skills relevant to growing portfolio companies. Chambers of commerce aligned with innovation goals.

Then comes infrastructure. Coworking spaces are built not just for startups, but for community workshops, entrepreneur-in-residence programs, and workforce training hubs. Transit that connects neighborhoods to opportunity zones. Broadband initiatives funded through public-private collaboration.

Then comes the cascade. Startups reinvest in local vendors. Investors sit on nonprofit boards. Exit liquidity gets recycled into regional angel groups. Suddenly, a $500,000 loan to a local robotics firm isn't just about getting paid back, it's about activating an entire network effect of prosperity.

This is what unlocking a regional ecosystem looks like.

Not every town needs to become a tech hub. But every region deserves the chance to participate in the upside of innovation. And it's the job of the capital stack to make that possible.

Venture isn't a geography anymore. It's a mindset. And it can show up wherever there are ambitious people and patient capital.

That's the kind of regeneration the Full-Stack Venture Capital Funds™ model enables. Because it provides not just the check but the context.

Why Capital Without Context Fails Communities

Too often, capital behaves like a tourist. It arrives with a camera, snaps a few pictures of local "innovation," drops off some funding, and leaves before the impact or the unintended consequences take hold. No roots. No staying power. No accountability.

This "flyover funding" model is especially pervasive in underserved and emerging markets. Investors chase "off-coastal" opportunities because the valuation arbitrage is attractive. But without context, without local partners, cultural intelligence, or operational infrastructure, they either overpromise, underdeliver, or simply extract.

That's not Venture Capital. That's venture colonialism.

Communities are not blank canvases for innovation. They are living, breathing networks of history, relationships, and informal economies. Injecting capital into that system without understanding it can disrupt more than it builds. Especially if the funding is conditional on exits that are misaligned with local business norms or timelines.

Here's a concrete example. A national VC firm funds a minority-owned food startup in Atlanta. They insist on "scaling fast" into other cities. But the founder's core revenue and cultural identity come from partnerships with Black-owned farms in the Southeast. Scaling too fast dilutes that authenticity, burns cash, and kills the business. Capital killed culture.

Or another: A rural Midwest startup gets equity funding for a high-tech logistics platform. But their real opportunity isn't in exit multiples. It's in solving local distribution bottlenecks for small agricultural producers, creating dozens of jobs in the process. A debt instrument, paired with long-term revenue sharing, would have been better for everyone. But that wasn't on the term sheet.

The point is this: context matters. Structure matters. The form of capital is just as important as its source.

And that's where the Full-Stack Venture Capital Funds™ model shines.

Because when you can meet a community where it is offering credit where banks won't, equity where angels can't, and revenue-based structures where exits are improbable, you stop guessing. You start designing capital around actual needs, not theoretical returns.

You become not just an investor, but a partner in community transformation.

A Community-Aligned Capital Stack in Practice

To really serve communities, especially those historically overlooked or underbanked, you can't just show up with a check and a camera crew. You need a toolkit. One that includes more than just equity, and more than just words.

Let's walk through what that looks like when done right.

Start with a founder in a midsize Southern city. She's a second-generation manufacturer of low-emission HVAC systems for mobile homes, which are common in her area. Her company is profitable but plateauing. She's too small for private equity, too old for venture, and too practical for a startup accelerator that wants her to pitch in San Francisco with vaporware and a hoodie.

Traditional VC wouldn't know where to start. Bank financing would balk at the asset-light model. But a full-stack venture capital partner sees the whole picture.

First, offer a revenue-based loan to help the company expand production capacity and hire two new welders. That gets the flywheel turning.

Next, provide structured equity for a new services division offering retrofitting and maintenance packages directly to trailer park operators. This diversifies revenue and creates recurring cash flow.

Finally, add a flexible line of credit to support working capital tied to new contracts. No personal guarantee, just a forward-looking underwriting of actual business health.

At each step, capital is aligned with use. It's matched to the risk. And it's timed to the business's own growth curve, not an artificial timeline imposed by fund mechanics.

The result?

The founder keeps majority ownership. Her team grows from 7 to 18. The company starts training local high school grads in fabrication through a partnership with the community college. And eventually, a regional strategic buyer makes an offer that reflects not just her EBITDA but the value of her community footprint.

That's what happens when capital behaves more like an architect and less like a speculator. You get durable businesses rooted in place. You get wealth that stays local. And you get founders who don't just "cash out," they build out.

From Extraction to Circulation

Most traditional funds extract value from the communities they invest in, where the upside looks best, reap the returns, and redeploy capital elsewhere. This is the default mode in globalized finance: move money to where it multiplies fastest, regardless of whose economy it helps or hurts.

But a Full-Stack Venture Capital Funds™ with an embedded income engine can shift the pattern from extraction to circulation.

When your capital stack includes dividend-paying assets, credit instruments with repayment, and patient equity, you don't have to exit a company to realize value. That means your investors get paid while the business stays in place, grows in place, and contributes in place.

This matters more than people realize. In traditional Venture Capital, the only way capital is returned is through a sale or an IPO, both of which often mean a company is uprooted. Jobs leave, headquarters move, and control drifts to whoever cut the biggest check. And all the local upside the economic velocity created by that company goes with it.

In a circular capital model, the outcomes are different. Take the example of a growing outpatient healthcare group in a regional city. A Full-Stack Venture Capital Funds™ can provide a blend of working capital, growth credit, and minority equity to help it scale. As the company grows, the credit is repaid, and interest is recycled. Income-generating components of the deal flow back to the fund as dividends. Equity remains patient, allowing for a strategic exit in 8 or 10 years rather than a rushed flip.

And during that time, the business is not pressured to relocate, slash headcount, or over-optimize for GAAP earnings to hit a quarterly mark. It can serve its community, train local staff, and actually deliver on the "impact" many funds claim without the capital structure to support it.

This isn't an argument for abandoning profit. It's an argument for recognizing that profit and place are not opposing forces; they're compounding forces when the incentives are aligned.

Local Wealth Is Venture Capital's Untapped Alpha

Venture Capital, at its best, has always been about catalyzing change. But too often, it's change imported from elsewhere and exported for someone else's benefit. The Full-Stack Venture Capital Funds™ model flips that script by embedding capital in the same places it expects returns. Not just by extracting from communities but by reinvesting in them.

BROKEN

What we've outlined in this chapter isn't a social mission disguised as an investment strategy. It's a smarter approach to allocating capital: one that strengthens the base where your portfolio operates, builds more resilient companies by keeping their roots intact, and creates wealth cycles that can actually be repeated.

In the end, the investors win, the founders win, and the communities win. That's not utopian thinking. That's simply what happens when financial tools are structured to stay longer, listen deeper, and align smarter.

Onward to the future.

Chapter 9

The Future of Venture Capital is Full-Stack Venture Capital Funds™

Part 1: The Limits of the Legacy Model

There's a saying in Venture Capital that "you're only as good as your top three exits." That worked fine when every other company was being bought at inflated multiples in under five years. But that era is over. And the old model, frankly, is showing its age like an out-of-shape sprinter being asked to run a marathon.

The traditional venture fund structure is deceptively simple: raise a fixed pool of money, deploy it across a portfolio of startups over a few years, then pray the exits hit before the fund clock runs out. The GP earns its management fees and carried interest. The LP waits. And waits. And waits.

Here's the problem: the waiting no longer works.

Post-2020, exit markets froze. IPOs evaporated. Strategic buyers grew cautious. Valuations compressed, but startup expectations didn't. And those 10-year fund lives started to feel like prison sentences for everyone involved. Even Investors with multi-billion-dollar portfolios got tired of seeing "Unrealized Gains" on yet another glossy pitch deck while their other private investments delivered real yield, real distributions, and real accountability.

On the founder side, things haven't been much better. Most were coached to view each round of equity as a ladder rung, climbing ever upward toward a mythical exit that starts with a "B". But what if there's no next round? What if the capital market window closes mid-ascent? Founders suddenly found themselves trapped unable to raise, unable to exit, burning through capital, and being asked to "just hold on" for a better market.

COMPARISON OF TRADITIONAL VC VS. FULL-STACK VC FUND

KEY COMPARISONS

ASPECT	TRADITIONAL VC	FULL-STACK VC BDC
Capital Deployment	Focuses on equity only investments	Uses a combination of equity, debt, and buyouts
Risk Profile	High-risk, high-reward, with significant volatility	More diversified risk across multiple asset types
Return Type	Exit-driven (IPOs or acquisitions)	Income generation, exits, and long-term growth
Flexibility	Limited flexibility in capital structure	Flexible across market cycles
Stage Focus	Primarily early-stage startups	Covers early, growth, and expansion stages

Side-by-side comparison of Traditional VC and Full-Stack VC Fund models, showing differences in capital deployment, risk profile, return types, flexibility, and stage coverage.

Worst of all, the traditional fund structure all but mandated these binary outcomes. You either hit it big, or you disappear from the spreadsheet. Slow, steady, and sensible weren't welcome in this version of Silicon Valley storytelling.

In truth, the entire structure has been built around what's easiest for the fund managers, not what's optimal for the capital or the company. The 2 and 20 model creates misalignment. The decade-long commitment locks in Investors with no guarantee of liquidity. The obsession with follow-on rounds and markups over fundamentals distorts capital allocation. And diversification, the supposed safeguard of venture portfolios, often masks a troubling sameness across asset type, stage, and sector.

We are now seeing the repercussions, high-profile down rounds. Unicorns shedding horns. Fund Managers are struggling to raise successor funds. Investors are allocating away from early-stage tech. The tide has gone out, and many boats were built for calm weather only.

This isn't a blip. It's a structural shift.

And the question is: will we adapt, or keep bailing water out of a leaky ship?

Part 2: The Rise of the Multi-Asset Archetype

As the cracks in the legacy model deepen, a new type of capital firm is quietly taking shape. It's not your grandfather's VC firm, nor is it a Wall Street buyout shop with a flashy new logo. It's something hybrid, something intentional, something built from the ground up to weather volatility and unlock new forms of value.

This is the Full-Stack Venture Capital Funds™, a full-stack capital provider that can write checks for equity, debt, preferred instruments, royalties, or structured hybrids, all under one roof and with a unified philosophy.

At its core, the Full-Stack Venture Capital Funds™ model doesn't seek to reinvent capital. It simply seeks to *deploy it more intelligently*.

Instead of swinging for the fences with every check, these firms build portfolios that blend:

- Early-stage equity for upside.

- Private credit for income and downside protection.

- Growth buyouts for accelerated returns and controlled exits.

- Revenue participation and dividend recap structures for liquidity before an exit.

In short, they've stopped trying to time liquidity events like a Las Vegas roulette wheel and started engineering them thoughtfully, deal by deal.

What makes this model powerful is how it compounds in multiple directions:

- For Investors, it delivers real cash-on-cash returns early and often.

- For founders, it reduces dilution and keeps control in the hands of operators.

- For the fund, it creates internal liquidity that can be recycled into more deals.

Even better, the toolkit is expansive. One company might use structured debt to finance a customer acquisition push. Another might convert part of a loan into equity after reaching a revenue milestone. A third might recap with a dividend model that delivers ongoing cash to investors without selling a single share.

This adaptability is no longer a luxury; it's becoming table stakes.

The next generation of top-tier firms will be those who can underwrite across the capital stack with rigor, deploy capital with flexibility, and govern with long-term alignment. Not just "Venture Capitalists" in the narrow sense, but "venture builders" who understand the entire lifecycle of company growth and have the financial tools to support it.

And when that capability exists in a single, integrated structure with common governance, shared deal teams, and clear reporting, it unlocks something far more powerful than just alpha.

It builds trust.

Because in this new model, investors don't just hope the next big exit is around the corner. They get paid to wait. Founders don't just hope their next round materializes. They get financed to reach real milestones. And communities don't just hope a company survives. They benefit from one that thrives with responsible, adaptive, and values-aligned capital.

WHAT INVESTORS WILL START DEMANDING

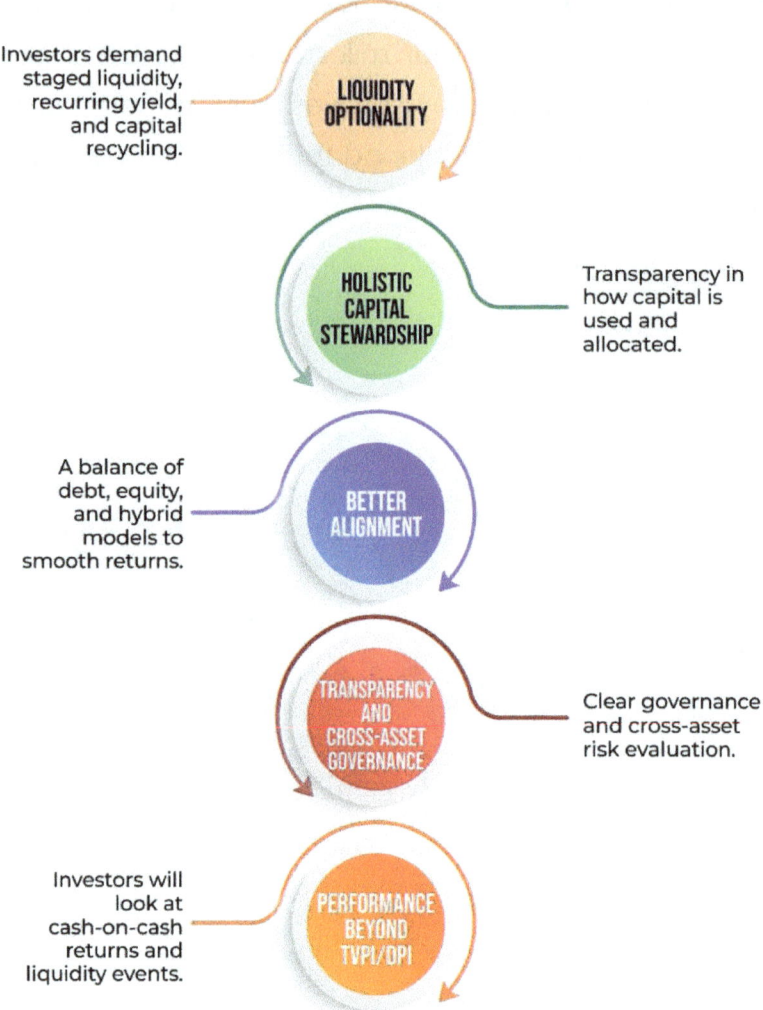

Investors demand staged liquidity, recurring yield, and capital recycling.

LIQUIDITY OPTIONALITY

HOLISTIC CAPITAL STEWARDSHIP

Transparency in how capital is used and allocated.

A balance of debt, equity, and hybrid models to smooth returns.

BETTER ALIGNMENT

TRANSPARENCY AND CROSS-ASSET GOVERNANCE

Clear governance and cross-asset risk evaluation.

Investors will look at cash-on-cash returns and liquidity events.

PERFORMANCE BEYOND TVPI/DPI

Emerging LP priorities: predictable liquidity, recurring yield, clearer governance, and balanced risk-return beyond TVPI/DPI.

This is the future of Venture Capital. And the future is multi-asset.

Part 3: What Investors Will Start Demanding

If there's one group that has quietly grown more vocal behind closed doors, it's the Investors. Pension funds, endowments, family offices, and institutional allocators aren't just chasing returns anymore; they're looking for durability, distribution, and discipline. The vintage VC model isn't failing because Investors are losing interest in venture. It's failing because it no longer meets their evolving standards for risk, liquidity, and transparency.

The Full-Stack Venture Capital Funds™ model is emerging not just because it's a better mousetrap for Fund Managers, but because Investors are beginning to demand it.

Here's what's happening across the capital landscape:

1. **Liquidity Optionality Is the New Gold Standard**

    Ten-year lockups with no interim distributions and only mark-to-model updates are becoming harder to justify. Investors are recalibrating their portfolios toward managers who can offer staged liquidity, recurring yield, or recycled capital events. A fund that can distribute current income even modestly stands out in a world where too many managers push off returns into perpetuity.

2. Holistic Capital Stewardship

Investors increasingly want to know: how is your capital actually being used? Are you bridging founders to scale or just marking up paper on SAFEs? Can you deploy capital in non-dilutive ways? Are you recycling proceeds to amplify returns? Full-Stack Venture Capital Funds™ has a clearer story to tell here. They aren't just participating, they're solving.

3. Better Alignment Through Blended Models

Pure equity portfolios tend to cluster risk at the same point in time: the exit. That creates portfolio-level volatility and misaligned timeframes. Blending income-producing instruments, senior secured debt, and structured equity allows for the smoothing of returns, greater capital recycling, and more predictable liquidity events. This, in turn, builds trust.

4. Transparency and Cross-Asset Governance

Sophisticated Investors want to see underwriting that works across the stack. They expect a valuation process that doesn't break when you introduce credit or royalties. They expect waterfall models that reward investors and founders proportionally and flexibly. And they expect governance that isn't biased by one asset type or another, but is designed to serve the portfolio as a whole.

5. Performance Beyond TVPI and DPI

While IRR, TVPI, and DPI remain the standard metrics, Investors are starting to look at more holistic markers: time to partial liquidity, cash-on-cash multiples, recycled capital rates, and even alignment scores. They want funds that can demonstrate value creation that's realized, not just theorized. Full-Stack Venture Capital Funds™ that include income and hybrid instruments can deliver these insights with more frequency and precision.

6. Fund Managers Who Think Like Asset Managers

Gone are the days when charisma and a compelling pitch deck alone could raise funds. Investors are demanding discipline: policies, procedures, risk frameworks, transparent reporting, and governance models that look more like those of an asset management firm than a startup incubator. Full-Stack Venture Capital Funds™ tends to attract operators and executives with crossover experience, and Investors are noticing.

Ultimately, Investors are not walking away from Venture Capital; they're evolving their expectations. They still want exposure to innovation, growth, and asymmetric upside. But they want it delivered in a framework that reflects modern risk realities, portfolio construction principles, and the sophistication they bring to other parts of their portfolio.

The Full-Stack Venture Capital Funds™ structure answers that call. It says: yes, you can have venture returns with greater control. Yes, you can have early distributions without sacrificing upside. Yes, you can support founders with smarter capital and still get paid while you wait.

That's what Investors are starting to demand. And the firms that meet that demand will own the next decade.

Part 4: Designing the New Standard

Designing a Full-Stack Venture Capital Funds™ isn't about bolting a credit arm onto a venture fund or sprinkling in private equity for flavor. It's about building an entirely new chassis, one that's engineered for durability, flexibility, and alignment from day one.

So what does that look like in practice?

1. Structure First, Style Second

Most venture funds start with a style: "We back seed-stage fintech founders," or "We focus on climate tech." But in a multi-asset world, structure comes first. Is this an evergreen vehicle? A BDC? A hybrid RIA model? What kind of regulatory framework does it operate under? What investor protections are baked in? These are not afterthoughts. They're the bones of the business.

2. Permanent Capital With Purpose

The idea isn't just to raise more money, it's to raise smarter money. By designing vehicles that allow for rolling closes, dividend policies, or income participation, fund managers can better match investor timelines with portfolio company needs. A BDC or evergreen model allows you to compound, recycle, and grow without being trapped in the artificial timing cycle of vintage funds. It also allows investors to stay in longer, capturing more upside on the backend while still receiving cash flow throughout.

3. Cross-Functional Investment Committees

When you're underwriting structured credit, growth equity, and early-stage venture in the same portfolio, you need diverse thinkers in the room. The IC must be designed for balance: some members trained in downside protection, others in upside-down pattern recognition. And they must be trained to speak a common valuation language. This is less about consensus and more about multidimensional judgment.

4. Portfolio Construction for Optionality

Most traditional VC funds cluster risk in a single mode: binary equity outcomes. The new standard spreads risk intelligently. For example:

- A third of capital might go into senior credit or revenue-based finance.

- A third into equity with downside protections (convertibles, preferred).

- A third into high-upside early-stage deals.

The result? Optionality. Liquidity events happen across time horizons. You're never dependent on any one exit. And you can make strategic decisions based on the broader environment, not just company-by-company timing.

5. Embedded Services, Not Just Capital

In the new standard, capital is the starting point, not the endpoint. Portfolio companies expect more than a check. They need help with valuation modeling, regulatory compliance, GTM strategies, financial projections, debt restructuring, and more. That means hiring internal talent, offering shared services, and building domain-specific playbooks that turn your capital into value far beyond the dollar amount.

6. Continuous Calibration

Full-Stack Venture Capital Funds™ live in a more complex world than pure-play strategies. As a result, their models must be reviewed and refined constantly. This includes:

- Adjusting allocation based on macro trends.

- Updating DCF and comparable models quarterly.

- Stress-testing for interest rate shifts or liquidity freezes.

- Revisiting team capacity and hiring based on service load.

Firms that succeed here don't just "set and forget." They operate like a cockpit, always flying with eyes on the instruments.

7. **Communication Built for Sophistication**

    Investors backing a Full-Stack Venture Capital Funds™ deserve more than canned quarterly updates and delayed K-1s. They want:

- Forward-looking dashboards

- Breakdowns by asset class, stage, and time to liquidity

- Income vs. unrealized return analytics

- Risk-weighted exposure maps

- Strategic memos alongside financial reporting

The more you behave like a public-company-grade asset manager, the more credibility you build with the institutional investor base. The new standard demands it.

8. Culture of Intellectual Integrity

When you sit across the capital stack, you also sit across different investment philosophies. It's easy for cognitive dissonance to creep in: are we growth investors or credit allocators? Are we playing offense or defense? The firms that win are the ones that don't let style bias cloud their judgment. They stick to first principles. They ask: What does the portfolio need? What does the company need? What delivers risk-adjusted return in this environment?

That kind of discipline is rare. But it's the defining trait of the Full-Stack Venture Capital Funds™ investor.

Epilogue

A Quiet Success – One Fund's Bold Bet on the Model

In a financial ecosystem still dominated by vintage cycles, overconcentration, and binary bets, one fund quietly decided to do things differently.

It didn't chase unicorns at frothy valuations. It didn't rely on a single exit to build the portfolio. And it didn't just write checks and hope for the best.

Instead, it built a structure that could withstand shocks, reward patience, and grow stronger over time. That fund is Capital Q° Ventures' flagship fund, Capital Q° Business Development Company (CAPQ BDC), a multi-asset, dividend-paying, founder-aligned investment vehicle operating under the 1940 Act as a Business Development Company.

It's not a hypothetical. It's not a whiteboard sketch. It's a real, functioning fund. And it's working.

Real-World Execution

CAPQ BDC was designed to take all the best lessons from venture capital, private credit, and private equity and fuse them into a new model. The fund makes structured loans, growth equity investments, and selectively participates in founder-led acquisitions and long-hold private equity deals. Some positions pay interest from day one. Others accrue value over time. Some are structured for current yield, others for backend upside. The diversity is by design.

And while returns are essential, they're not the only measure. The fund has invested in companies that create jobs, anchor communities, and build resilience in sectors often overlooked by traditional VCs. From robotics and waste-to-energy tech to branded retail and healthcare infrastructure, CAPQ BDC shows that you can invest for impact without sacrificing return.

Dividend-Paying and Evergreen by Design

CAPQ BDC isn't built to exit fast; it's built to endure. That means paying current income to investors while holding longer for venture upside. That means using credit instruments to efficiently recycle capital. And that means treating liquidity not as an event, but as a feature of the fund itself.

Over time, this model rewards long-term holders with both cash flow and appreciation. The longer an investor stays in, the more they benefit from both early income and late-stage exits. In a world where most Investors are stuck waiting 10 years for the scoreboard, this fund delivers transparency, tempo, and total return.

Governance That Reflects the Mandate

This isn't a "friends and family" fund with ad hoc oversight. CAPQ BDC is governed by an independent board, regularly audited, and valued under IPEV standards. It employs professional administration, NAV reporting, and rigorous underwriting across asset types. It acts like an institution because it is one.

And yet, it remains deeply human. Founder calls aren't rushed. Follow-on decisions aren't reactive. Capital is deployed with purpose, not pressure.

A Model for the Future

Most importantly, this isn't a one-off. It's a blueprint.

Any firm willing to step out of the vintage cycle, align incentives across stakeholders, and operate with transparency and creativity can build something similar. The hard part is having the discipline to do it. But if you do, the upside is extraordinary.

Not just for investors. Not just for founders. But for the communities these companies serve, the families they employ, and the innovations they bring to life.

B R O K E N

This is the future of Venture Capital formation. It's quieter. More thoughtful. More durable. And it's already here.

www.ingramcontent.com/pod-product-compliance
Lightning Source LLC
Chambersburg PA
CBHW070019120726
47909CB00003B/994